W9-BZX-320

FROST

FROST

NICOLE LUIKEN

GREAT PLAINS
PUBLICATIONS

Copyright © 2007 Nicole Luiken Humphrey

Great Plains Publications
420 – 70 Arthur Street
Winnipeg, MB R3B 1G7
www.greatplains.mb.ca

All rights reserved. No part of this publication may be reproduced or transmitted in
any form or in any means, or stored in a database and retrieval system, without the
prior written permission of Great Plains Publications, or, in the case of photocopying
or other reprographic copying, a license from Access Copyright (Canadian Copyright
Licensing Agency), 1 Yonge Street, Suite 1900, Toronto, Ontario, Canada, M5E 1E5.

Great Plains Publications gratefully acknowledges the financial support provided
for its publishing program by the Government of Canada through the Book Publishing
Industry Development Program (BPIDP); the Canada Council for the Arts; as well
as the Manitoba Department of Culture, Heritage and Tourism; and the Manitoba
Arts Council.

Design & Typography by Relish Design Studios Ltd.

Printed in Canada by Friesens

CANADIAN CATALOGUING IN PUBLICATION DATA

Main entry under title:

Luiken, Nicole
    Frost / Nicole Luiken.

A novel.
    ISBN 978-1-894283-72-4

    I. Title
PS8573.U534F76 2007   jC813'.54   C2007-900429-6

AUTHOR'S NOTE

The real Iqaluit Airbase closed in 1992 and has not been reopened as of this publishing. The international crisis between North and South Korea is also fictionalized.

ACKNOWLEDGEMENTS:

Thanks to my brother Wayne for pointing out the flaw in the first draft ending of this novel. Thanks to my sister Sharna for helping me to make Kathy a stronger character. Thanks to my editor, Anita Daher, and the various members of my writer's group who critiqued the novel: Aaron V. Humphrey, Susan McFadzen, Karen Glessing, Marg DeMarco. Thanks also to Simon Adams for the information on Iqaluit Minor Hockey. All mistakes are, of course, mine.

To my four-year-old son, Luke, who also loves to type on the computerrrrrrrrrrrrrrrrrrrrrrrrrrrrrrrrrrrrrrrrrrrrrrrrrrrrrrrrrrrr rrrrrrrrrrrrrrrrrrrrrrrrrrrrrrrrrrrrrrrrrrrrrrrrrrrrrrrrrrrrrrrrrrrrrrrrrrrr rrrrrrrrrrrrrrrrrrrrrrrrrrrrrrrrrrrrrrrrrrrrrrrrrrrrrrrrrrrrrr

CHAPTER 1

-10 °C (+14 °F)

YOU KNOW WHAT YOU HAVE TO DO.

Johnny opened up the throttle further as the cold voice scratched at the door to his mind. He wished he could lock out the voice, but all he could do was ignore it. The snowmobile whizzed over a small hill and plunged down the other side, almost but not quite, airborne.

Behind him Kathy shouted with glee and held him tighter.

It was a perfect day. Crisp, but not too cold, no snowfall, with enough cloud to prevent snow glare, little wind.

You won't like what will happen if you don't listen to me, Johnny.

The words entered Johnny's mind as if drilled by an ice pick. He flinched, then opened up the throttle wider to drown the voice out.

He concentrated on the white open spaces ahead of him. Tundra, not fields. No trees, because Baffin Island was north of the treeline, and no hidden barbwire fences either. Just miles and miles of white until you hit the ocean. Or the mountains.

"Hey!" Kathy shouted over the throb of the motor. "Can I take another turn driving?"

The opportunity was too good to pass up. Johnny twisted his head around. "Sure," he said. The other girls in their snowmobiling party didn't drive much. It took a lot of upper arm strength to take a heavy snowmobile up a sharp incline. Kathy had the musculature—

she wanted to be a jet fighter pilot and lifted weights three times a week—but no snowmobile of her own.

Johnny eased off the throttle, and the snowmobile slid to a stop. He waited for her to get off, body tense.

Kathy swung one leg over the snowmobile, but Johnny's face must have given him away because she hesitated. "Wait. Is this one of your practical jokes? If I get off, are you going to drive away and leave me standing here?"

"No," Johnny said, forcing a grin.

She was still suspicious. "You get off first."

Instead Johnny opened up the throttle and sent the snowmobile leaping forward. Kathy shrieked and almost fell, but hung on, yelling and laughing at the same time. To her it was just a game.

For Johnny it was something very different. He wanted her off the snowmobile, but he dared not insist. Dared not draw Frost's attention to her.

Frost in his head, echoing in his skull.

You will do it, Johnny.

Under his winter jacket, Johnny shuddered.

Not now, he pleaded. Not yet.

Johnny would give in eventually, as he always had. He knew what Frost was capable of. Frost would kill, coldly and without remorse.

Johnny had already given up so much, including his brother and his last girlfriend, all for Frost's threats. This time was harder. Frost was asking him to give up his dream.

It's just for the season, he told himself. Next year you can do what you want. But the cold hollow feeling in his gut said differently.

You know what you have to do, Johnny.

Yes. He knew. Johnny did it.

CHAPTER 2

-10 °C (+14 °F)

AFTERWARD, WHAT KATHY REMEMBERED most vividly about the accident was the stranger's face.

Kathy had closed her eyes as they zoomed along, partly against the spray of snow, but mostly so she could glory in the feeling of speed.

It was almost like flying.

Her arms were tight around Johnny's chest, her head tucked to one side. She wished Johnny would let her take another turn, but he loved to drive just as much as she did. The next time they stopped she would ask his brother, Evan, if she could drive his snowmobile. He was the only one in their party not already riding double, and he probably wouldn't mind.

The engine whined suddenly, straining to go up the steep hill. They slowed. The snow ahead of them was trackless and pure. No other snowmobiles had been this way.

"Maybe I should get off," Kathy yelled near Johnny's ear.

"Nah, we can make it." Johnny opened up the throttle wider, and the snowmobile jumped ahead.

Kathy squinted, trying to see how far they had to go, but only saw white. She dared not tip her head back for fear of shifting her weight on the machine.

"Almost there," Johnny said. "Almost—"

The stranger appeared out of nowhere, on foot, almost directly in front of them. *Where the heck did he come from?*

Time seemed to slow as the stranger's eyes met hers for an instant. They were as dark and deep as the abyss. It was as if in one glance, he stripped her back to her most unlovely years. She felt thirteen again, gauche, shy, ungainly, the one the junior high boys called Giraffe.

She felt cold down to her soul.

As quickly as it had settled upon her, his gaze flicked past her, dismissed her as scenery. When he looked away, Kathy felt relief, as if a pressure had eased, but her joy in the day seemed suddenly flat, hammered thin.

The stranger's hair was silver, in sharp contrast to his eyes, which seemed to soak up the light. He watched Johnny like as a hawk might watch its prey. Kathy had the stomach-churning sensation of being caught up in a powerful current...

The snowmobile engine gave a sudden whine and died.

The stranger smiled, exposing sharp teeth.

Momentum gone, the snowmobile began to tip over backwards. There was a half second when Johnny might have kept the machine from flipping, but in the instant's panic he turned and grabbed Kathy instead, rolling her off the seat and into the snow, before the snowmobile could fall on them and crush them.

The impact with the ground drove the air from Kathy's lungs. Cold snow hit her in the face, momentarily blinding her.

Together Kathy and Johnny rolled down the hill in a mad flurry of arms and legs, snow and sky, before stopping about one-third of the way down. The snowmobile wasn't as fortunate. It kept tumbling, performing a slow somersault, spraying snow, heading for a large boulder close to the bottom. It was mid-October, and the snowfall was still a fairly thin covering over the stark stone of the Canadian Shield. The snowmobile hit the rock with a bang. Kathy winced at the sound of machinery breaking.

Abruptly, she remembered the stranger. A terrible thought occurred to her. "We didn't hit him, did we?" As soon as she asked the question, she knew that they couldn't have. The last thing she'd seen was him smiling.

"Are you okay?" Johnny leaned down to ask her. His usually laughing green eyes were serious.

"Oh, yeah. I'm tough." Which was true, even if unfeminine. Kathy got to her feet without help. The red winter jacket and ski-pants she was wearing had cushioned her fall, but she felt bruised, and her left cheek stung as if it had been rug-burned. "How about you?"

Johnny shrugged. "I've been slammed around worse playing hockey. Are you sure you're okay?"

"Yes." Kathy took off her helmet and began to brush away the snow that had jammed inside before all of it melted in her hair, then didn't know why she'd bothered. Her brown hair hung in sweaty tangles, beyond help—Kathy considered helmet hair to be the price she paid for speed. Though today was the first time she had really needed her helmet. The first accident she had been in.

She looked around for the stranger, but didn't see him. Just the thought of him smiling while they flipped made her furious. Where had he gone?

Johnny distracted her by hugging her and kissing her forehead. "I'm an idiot. Tell me I'm an idiot."

"You're an idiot."

"And a jerk."

"And a jerk," Kathy repeated obediently.

Still Johnny didn't smile. "I should have known that slope was too steep for two people. You could have been hurt."

"But I wasn't." Johnny's obvious concern warmed Kathy. Sometimes Kathy worried that Johnny treated her more like a buddy than a girlfriend. "We're both okay. That's the important part. Right?"

"Right." Johnny gave her an affectionate squeeze.

The rest of the snowmobiling party began to zoom back over the hill, having missed them. Minik Ashevak and Brendan Robertson, members of Johnny's hockey team, were followed by their girlfriends, Cheryl Meekitjuk and Tracy Beaumont, and also Johnny's younger brother Evan.

There was an immediate babble of voices. What had happened, were they all right, thank goodness it was only the snowmobile that had been damaged.

Evan had a different opinion; he stared down at the wreck in morbid fascination. "Uncle Dan is going to kill you," he told Johnny.

"He'd only just paid it off." Evan's shoulders straightened. "I'll tell him I did it."

Kathy was puzzled by his offer and unsurprised when Johnny refused.

"No, it's my fault. I'll take the blame."

"But—"

"No, Evan," Johnny said firmly. "Leave Uncle Dan to me." He grinned and kicked snow at the snowmobile. "See, it's not as bad as it looks. It's just a little dinged up. Maybe he won't notice."

The corners of Kathy's mouth twitched. Dinged up was a gross understatement, and Johnny knew it. The snowmobile was totalled: one ski broken off, the handlebars wrenched askew, the body dented, and the tail pipe knocked off.

❄ ❄ ❄ ❄

His uncle noticed.

His uncle could hardly have failed to notice when it took two snowmobiles to drag the broken snowmobile into his yard. He came out and watched as they maneuvered it around the water and sewage pipes. The town of Iqaluit was built on permafrost, so pipes had to be aboveground. Since the town was above the tree-line most of the houses were pre-fabricated—built elsewhere and shipped in parts.

Even in a good mood Dan Vander Zee was a brusque man, not given to talking or smiling; the only similarity Kathy had ever seen between him and Johnny was height. They were both tall.

"Was this your doing?" Dan Vander Zee asked Johnny, tight-lipped.

"Yes." Briefly, Johnny explained about the steep hill and the double load. "It was my fault."

"I'm sure it was," his uncle said coldly. "This is the absolute last straw, Johnny. When I took the job in Iqaluit this spring, you and I made a deal. You would behave in a responsible manner, and I would let you accept the invitation to play for one of the junior hockey teams down south. You give me no choice. You're staying in Iqaluit for the winter."

Evan looked miserable. Now Kathy understood why he had volunteered to take the blame. Hockey meant everything to Johnny, the same way the dream of being a jet fighter pilot drove Kathy.

He drilled relentlessly, in season and out. He was hoping to be drafted into the NHL in a couple of years. A season of only playing on Iqaluit's local team would set him back.

Teams in Iqaluit played mostly with each other—the Women's team vs. PeeWees, Bantams/Midgets vs. Senior Mens, etc. There were no roads out of Iqaluit, not even elsewhere on the island, and airfare to other northern communities was expensive. Iqaluit hosted several tournaments every year and sent its best players to play on Team Baffin at Territorials in Yellowknife, but that was the extent of outside competition.

Johnny's face was very pale. "I understand."

For a moment Dan Vander Zee's face softened, then the lines bracketing his mouth deepened. "You brought this on yourself."

"I'm sorry," Johnny said sincerely.

His words angered his uncle all over again. "Are you? It's not just the machine—though if it wasn't insured I'd damn well be taking the four thousand dollars out of your inheritance money—it's the risk you took. Not just with your own life, but with your passenger. Kathy could have been hurt, do you understand that?"

Johnny closed his eyes. Nodded.

"It wasn't Johnny's fault." Kathy came to his defence. "It was the stranger. He startled us."

Johnny was shaking his head. "What stranger?"

"The man on the hill. You must have seen him," Kathy insisted. "He was only five feet away from us when we flipped. He was staring at you. He had silver hair and dark eyes. Cold looking." She shivered.

Johnny shrugged helplessly. "Sorry."

Kathy felt herself growing desperate. She appealed to the group. "One of you must have seen him when you came back down the slope." She hadn't seen the stranger after the accident and had assumed he'd vanished over the hill. He'd been on foot and couldn't have gotten far.

Minik shrugged.

"Sorry," Evan said.

Cheryl, Brendan, and Tracy shook their heads. No one had seen him.

How could they not have seen him? Were they blind?

"Was he Inuit?" Evan asked, trying to be helpful.

"No." Kathy shook her head. The stranger's skin had been almost ivory, but when she tried to remember what he'd been wearing, she drew a blank. She hadn't been able to tear her gaze away from his eyes.

Kathy bit her lip, upset without really knowing why. If the stranger's surprise appearance hadn't caused the snowmobile accident, it hardly mattered if anyone else had seen him. She let the subject drop.

❄ ❄ ❄ ❄

Kathy had seen Frost. This was very bad.

Johnny regretted not pushing her off the snowmobile when he had the chance—but he'd been afraid that if he did so Frost might think that Kathy was important to Johnny. He'd thought he could protect her better if she was closer. And he had. She wasn't hurt.

But she'd seen Frost. A bad thing. For Kathy more than for Johnny.

CHAPTER 3

-12 °C (+11 °F)

KATHY DIDN'T UNDERSTAND IT. Johnny was acting as if nothing had happened, as if he didn't care that he wouldn't be playing junior hockey.

"You see?" Smiling, Johnny punched Evan's shoulder when their uncle went back inside the house. "That wasn't so bad."

While they all stared, he kept talking. "Are you coming to the game tonight, Kathy? We're going to kick butt, right guys?"

Slowly, Minik, Brendan and Evan chimed in. "Right, Johnny."

"Of course, I'll come," Kathy said, desperate to show support even though Johnny was pretending he didn't need it.

"How about you two?" Johnny asked the other two girls.

"I'll be there," Cheryl said.

"Sorry, I can't make it." Tracy made a face, wrinkling up her freckled nose."I've got relatives in town."

Oh, great. Kathy liked Brendan's girlfriend, Tracy. Minik's girlfriend, Cheryl, was an entirely different prospect. And they would have to sit together; there was no way around it. The guys would expect it.

✳✳✳✳

The game started at 7:00 p.m., but the guys went in early to dress, leaving Kathy and Cheryl alone in the bleachers.

Cheryl was an Inuit girl with chin-length black hair and a round face. When she smiled she was rather pretty, but she stopped smiling as soon as she and Kathy were alone. Without Tracy to act as their buffer, they had nothing to say to each other.

What could she say to someone who wanted her boyfriend? Kathy avoided eye contact. Cheryl was dating Minik now, but she'd dated Johnny before that.

Kathy didn't know how long Johnny and Cheryl had dated or why they broke up. They'd already been history when Kathy first met Johnny—and he'd proposed.

It had happened during her second week at school. Sink or swim week, was how Kathy thought of it, after having gone through the experience half a dozen times whenever her dad was transferred to another Canadian Forces base. The first week in a new school everyone was curious and friendly; the second week everyone would make up their minds. Was the new girl from Alberta a loser or nice? The second week everyone knew her name, but she knew barely anyone.

When Johnny had called her name in the hallway, she hadn't glanced up, certain he must be talking to another Kathy. Evan happened to be her Chemistry 20 partner. She thought this might be Evan's older brother, but they had never been introduced. She would have remembered. Johnny was cute.

"Kathy!" he called again, and when she paused, confused, he dropped to his knees in front of her in the hallway. "Will you marry me?"

Her mind went utterly blank; she just stood there, gaping like a fish. Johnny took advantage of her stillness and kissed her hand. Actually kissed it, his lips brushing her knuckles. "Sweetheart. Darling." He stared up at her with a totally straight face. "Please say you will. I'll climb a thousand mountains, swim the ocean if you will but marry me."

Bright pink, she tried to tug her hand away and failed. It felt like the whole school stopped what they were doing and looked on in amusement. "No!" she cried, finally.

"No?" Johnny clutched his heart as if wounded, eliciting another round of laughter.

Kathy found herself apologizing. "I'm really sorry, but—"

Johnny bounced back to his feet. "In that case how about a date Friday night? Eight o'clock. I'll pick you up." He strolled away before she had a chance to open her mouth.

The proposal had been a bet, of course, but Johnny could have proposed to any girl. He had picked her. Too-tall Kathy O'Dwyer of the ordinary brown hair and ordinary blue eyes.

The date wasn't part of the bet; it was strictly Johnny's idea. It had gone surprisingly well. Johnny's outrageous teasing had relaxed Kathy out of most of her nervousness by the time the movie was over.

Only later, hanging around on the street outside the theater, had Kathy felt uncomfortable when Cheryl had come up to Johnny, a very intense look on her face. She ignored Kathy. "You're really doing this then?" she asked. "You're really dating her?"

Johnny spoke with utmost gentleness. "We broke up, Cheryl. I'm with Kathy now."

"Then you're an idiot." Cheryl turned on her heel and left.

A week later Cheryl had cold-bloodedly started dating Minik. He was friends with Johnny; dating Minik made Cheryl part of their group.

What Minik, a basically nice guy, saw in Cheryl, Kathy could not fathom. Okay, that wasn't strictly true. Personally, she thought Cheryl was sullen, but Kathy could see that the other girl also had an intensity and a sultriness that Kathy could never match.

Cheryl took out a bag of muktuk—whale blubber mixed with berries—ate some, and wordlessly held out the bag to Kathy.

"No, thank you," Kathy said politely, hiding an inward shudder. Kathy did not have a very adventuresome palate; the Inuit "country" food of raw seal or caribou meat and blubber grossed her out. She wasn't proud of the fact, but she couldn't help it. Knowing intellectually that raw meat had more vitamins than cooked meat and had allowed the Inuit to survive the long Arctic winter without dying of scurvy, didn't stop her stomach from rolling over at the thought—and she suspected Cheryl knew it.

It was cold in the stands, and Kathy was shivering by the time the Bantam and Old-timer teams skated out. The crowd came to its feet, whistling and clapping both home teams. A wave of Johnny's hand rewarded Kathy as he flashed past on silver skates. Number 19, star center. His sweater read J. Vander Zee to distinguish him from Evan, who played defence.

Minik followed. Cheryl cheered her boyfriend, too, but, to Kathy's ears, no more than she'd cheered anyone else. Brendan was scratching up the ice in front of his net and talking to Evan.

Circling completed, the ref blew the whistle, and Johnny skated up for the face-off. He won it, passing the puck back to Minik, his left winger. Their line skated forward across the blue line. Crowded by a defenceman, Minik passed the puck to Johnny. The puck flew to his stick as if magnetized.

Another defenceman blocked Johnny's way, but he deked neatly around him and took a quick wristshot on goal, aiming the puck like a missile at the top left corner of the net. The goalie caught a corner of it, but it tumbled off his glove and into the net. The red light flashed and the buzzer sounded. He'd scored! And only 32 seconds had passed on the clock.

Kathy cheered wildly. Before dating Johnny, she'd only watched occasional games during the Stanley Cup playoffs; she'd been surprised how much more involving it was at an actual game rather than watching it on TV.

That night Johnny played like a demon. He was a higher caliber player than the rest of his team and generally scored at least two goals or assists per game. That night he scored a natural hat-trick—three goals in a row.

Kathy yelled herself hoarse.

Cheryl was less impressed. When Johnny stole the puck yet again, she scowled and stood up. "That's it." Cheryl made her way down the stands toward the player's box and waited until Johnny piled onto the bench and guzzled water.

While Kathy stared at her in disbelief, Cheryl started to harangue Johnny. From two rows up Kathy could hear her voice perfectly. "Stop it, Johnny. Just stop it. We know you can score whenever you want. We get it. Let everyone else play, too."

Instead of telling her off, Johnny blinked. "Sorry," he said humbly. "I got lost in the game. It just felt so good, you know?"

Cheryl nodded brusquely and came back up to sit by Kathy. Neither of them said a word. Kathy seethed. Johnny had just suffered a major disappointment today. Wasn't he entitled to a little fun?

Johnny did tone it down over the next two periods. He still skated like a maniac after the puck, as if his career depended on him reaching it first, but he started passing more and, she swore, practising difficult backhand shots. He got one more goal and two assists.

Thanks to Johnny the Bantams won 8 to 4. The guys should have been exhausted, but they never were after a win.

Hair still wet from the shower, Johnny came out of the locker room and hugged her. With his arm around Kathy's waist, Johnny and the others trooped outside. "So where's the party?" Johnny asked.

"My house," Brendan said. "My parents are playing mah-jong next door and they said I could invite a few people over."

"You coming, Kathy?" Johnny asked.

Kathy hesitated. She'd been planning to go straight home. She knew that if she told Johnny she wanted to get up early tomorrow to train he would understand.

Most people looked at her as if she were crazy when she explained how much time she dedicated to keeping fit and getting good grades now so that in five years when she'd graduated from university she had a chance of being accepted into the Armed Forces. Ambition was the major thing she and Johnny had in common. Johnny was just as dedicated to his hockey career as she was to fighter jets—he just needed less sleep.

But now Johnny's career plans had suffered a major setback. Kathy didn't understand how he could want to go to a party. If Kathy had just been rejected by the Armed Forces she would have wanted to be alone to lick her wounds.

The idea that Johnny might need her made Kathy change her mind. "Just for a couple of hours."

"Great." Johnny smiled at her as if her presence really mattered to him. "Let's go."

Everyone piled into Johnny and Evan's old beater of a car. Cars were still a bit of a rarity on Baffin Island. In the summer everyone drove quads; in the winter the parking lots were full of snowmobiles, often ferrying whole families.

Johnny usually drove, but his uncle had taken away his driving privileges so he gave up his seat to Evan. Kathy ended up scrunched between the two brothers while Minik, Cheryl and Brendan sat in the back. They'd been known to squish Tracy in, too.

Minik and Cheryl necked while Brendan tactfully looked out the window. Johnny listened to the car stereo and restlessly drummed on his legs. Kathy stared straight ahead at the lacy curtain of falling snow, careful not to look at Evan.

For the last couple weeks Kathy had felt uneasy around Evan, and she didn't know why.

In some ways Evan was a quieter, more serious, version of Johnny. Both brothers had short brown hair, Johnny's leaning perhaps a little bit more towards chestnut, with a few red highlights in the sun. They were both tall, but Johnny was two inches taller at 6'4". They both played hockey, but Johnny was the star. They were both cute, but Johnny was cuter. Johnny was the life of the party; Evan was not. Johnny was a speed demon; Evan drove as if expecting to hit a caribou at any second—which, to be fair, was known to happen in Iqaluit. Johnny got B's and C's in school; Evan got mostly A's and B's. Johnny was popular; Evan was more comfortable in the background. Like Kathy was.

Evan reminded her how unalike she and Johnny were, which was stupid. Opposites were supposed to attract.

Kathy turned and smiled at Johnny. She hung onto her smile for the next couple of hours.

She'd been hoping to talk to Johnny at the party, but Brendan's idea of "a few people" appeared to be different from her own—and, she suspected, his parents. The whole hockey team was there, and it was a zoo.

A whirlwind swept up Johnny as soon as he was in the door. Or maybe Johnny was the whirlwind. Kathy tagged along for a while, but soon gave up and sat down. She felt stupid. Why had she ever thought Johnny needed her tonight? He was obviously fine.

Johnny was coming to her house for Thanksgiving tomorrow. Kathy consoled herself that she'd have him to herself then.

An hour later Kathy sneaked a glance at her watch. Only eleven-thirty. Still a bit early to ask to go home, especially since Evan would have to drive. She tapped her toe in time to the music blasting from the stereo. She was bored. Time to go find Johnny, maybe ask him to dance. Restlessly, she got to her feet.

She almost collided with Evan, and the drink in his hand sloshed. Kathy would bet that he was drinking plain cola. Although Iqaluit was a controlled community with no liquor stores, someone always managed to sneak some alcohol to the party. This time it was a mickey of rye, but Evan took his responsibility for driving seriously.

"Sorry," he said. "I didn't spill on you, did I?"

"No."

"Good."

An awkward silence fell. Kathy felt nervous and clumsy.

"So how are you feeling?" Evan asked. "That was a heck of a tumble you guys took this afternoon."

"I'm fine. Just some bruises." Another silence fell. Kathy looked over Evan's shoulder again for Johnny, about to make her excuses.

"Listen," Evan said, "I'm a little worried about Johnny's reaction to not being allowed to play junior hockey."

Kathy grimaced. "You mean his non-reaction."

"Yeah." Evan looked down at his hands and then up again. "He's been talking about playing junior hockey for months. I can't believe he didn't even argue with Uncle Dan."

Kathy couldn't believe it either. "Maybe he's just biding his time until your uncle cools down," she offered.

Evan nodded. "That's probably it." He didn't look convinced.

An awkward silence fell. Kathy changed the subject. "Have you seen Johnny? I was just going to ask him to dance."

"He's over in the corner." Evan pointed to a knot of laughing people.

She should have known—follow the sound of fun and there's Johnny. Kathy smiled her thanks and started to edge sideways through the crowd.

"Wait." Evan caught her arm. He smiled nervously. "Johnny won't dance this one. Why don't you dance with me?"

Kathy frowned. "Why wouldn't Johnny dance this one?" She knew he liked the song Winter of My Heart.

"Uh, never mind, I shouldn't have said anything."

"But you did."

Evan sighed. "It was Johnny and Cheryl's song, that's all."

"And you don't think he would dance it with me." Tiny claws of jealousy pricked Kathy. She and Johnny didn't have a special song.

Evan looked trapped. "I don't—"

"Well, let's find out." Kathy plowed a path straight towards Johnny. Cheryl was watching Johnny, an expression of bittersweet yearning on her face. Johnny didn't seem to be aware of the music at all, joking with Minik and Brendan. Kathy smiled determinedly at him. "Dance with me?" She held out her hand in challenge.

"Dance? The lady wishes to dance?" Johnny asked theatrically. "Then dance she shall. Stop the music!" Commandingly, Johnny held up his hand until someone shut off the CD player. "We must tango!" He grabbed Kathy close and stalked with her across the room. "Da, da, da, da-da, da, da."

People started to clap in the rhythm of a tango.

They switched direction and stalked back the other way.

Johnny dipped Kathy low as she laughed helplessly. He began to ham it up even more. Lacking a rose, he snatched up a plastic straw and held it in his teeth. He wiggled his eyebrows at her in a mock leer.

Kathy was breathless when they finished the tango. And reassured. It wasn't until her curfew rolled around and Evan chauffeured her and Johnny to her house that it occurred to her that Johnny hadn't danced his and Cheryl's song with her.

The thought leached away some of her happiness as they were waved past the guard onto the army base.

Evan looked politely away while Johnny walked Kathy to her door, but she still felt self-conscious and was glad when Johnny only gave her a brief kiss. They leaned foreheads together, an ancient custom, Johnny had once assured her. It meant, "I like you better than fish."

Kathy watched him go. The question was, did Johnny like her better than Cheryl?

❄ ❄ ❄ ❄

Evan looked at Johnny when he climbed back in the car. "I suppose you want to go back to the party?" He sounded resigned to his older brother's foolishness.

"Yep." Johnny smiled. "Gotta celebrate."

"Celebrate," Evan repeated, and Johnny knew he was thinking about the chance Johnny had lost this afternoon.

"I'm the party man," Johnny said lightly, because he couldn't stand for Evan to bring up Uncle Dan and junior hockey. Besides, he did have things to celebrate. Not the hockey victory, but the fact that Kathy hadn't been hurt, and that none of Frost's threats were going to come to pass because Johnny had done what he was told.

Evan snorted. "You're not a party man, you're a candle burning at both ends," he said bluntly.

Johnny said nothing. Evan didn't understand. Johnny had to burn to stay warm, to keep the bone-deep cold away.

"I'm going to head home," Evan said when they had arrived back at Brendan's. "Do me a favour and don't stay too long, okay? You know it drives Aunt Pat crazy when you're out late."

"No later than two," Johnny lied.

Evan rolled his eyes. "Which means three at the earliest. See you tomorrow." He leaned over and gave Johnny's shoulder a friendly punch.

Johnny felt tears prick his eyes at the simple gesture. Sometime when he wasn't looking, Evan had forgiven Johnny's latest betrayal. Johnny wanted to put his arm around his brother's neck, but he was afraid. *Don't be too obvious*, he thought. *Don't let Frost know how much you care.*

He got out of the car and went in to the party.

Within seconds he knew it was safe. He felt both relief and disappointment: Cheryl had already left.

CHAPTER 4

-13 °C (+10 °F)

SOME NIGHTS CHERYL COULD CONVINCE herself she was over Johnny, but not tonight. Tonight it was as if Raven stood on her shoulder, claws digging deep, mocking her: *If you are over him, then why were you so angry when Kathy asked him to dance to your song? Why do you want to leave the party now that he's gone?*

Her reasons didn't matter. She was going home, that was all.

Cheryl told Minik where she was going, before slipping out. Minik nodded without taking his eyes off the Inuit-style wrestling contest going on in one corner. He was the next competitor.

It was only about ten blocks from Brendan's house, where the party was, to Cheryl's, hardly worth driving in this weather, but Cheryl knew that if she and Johnny had been going out, he would have insisted she be driven.

When they'd broken up, Cheryl hadn't cried. In some odd way she'd anticipated their breakup, expected it. When, three hours later, Johnny had proposed to Kathy O'Dwyer in the hallway, Cheryl had understood intuitively that asking Kathy out had merely been Johnny's way of distancing himself from Cheryl.

The poor kid had had no idea how to take Johnny. What Kathy should have done was look at him, absolutely deadpan, and say, "Where's the ring?" or, "I like diamonds, are you sure you can afford me?" anything but just blush and stare like she had.

Cheryl hadn't thought they would last, but it was over a month now, and they were still dating.

Snow crunched under her boots as she walked. It had snowed earlier and was probably still cloudy—the temperature hadn't dropped as much as it should have if the sky had cleared off.

Cheryl walked alone, unafraid of the dark. The streetlights made it too light for her taste, and she wished for a moment that she were still living in the small community of 400 people where she had grown up, rather than in 5000-plus Iqaluit.

Iqaluit was the capital of Nunavut and the largest place Cheryl had ever been. The thought of living in a city like Montreal with a population of over three million made her shudder—the entire territory of Nunavut had a population of around 26,000—especially tonight when she longed to be out on the tundra, just she and the dogs and the snow sliding under the sled...

After Johnny broke up with her, Cheryl had skipped school for three days and done exactly that. For three days the closest she'd come to seeing another human being was a large stone inuksuk, piled up to resemble the figure of a man and to point the way.

Her Aunt Wanda had shaken her head at her, but her grandfather had understood and told her aunt, "Let the girl alone. The land heals."

Aunt Wanda waitressed at the Regency Frobisher Inn and firmly believed that the Inuit needed to look forward, not back into the past. "You want to go back to the days when the old would ask to be left alone to die so the others might have enough food to survive in the starving times? You want that?"

Cheryl didn't want to go back, but she also saw much in the traditional ways that she valued. The old ways had saved her.

When she was twelve and the Year of the Three Funerals had left her raw with grief, her grandfather had taken her out onto the land for two months and taught her the old ways. From him she had learned how to fish for Arctic char, build a snow house and mush a dog team. Grandfather trained sled dogs and had an old-fashioned suspicion of snowmobiles: "If you're stuck in a blizzard for four days, you can't eat a snowmobile."

Grandfather had saved her from the sullen, addicted girl she had been. She was strong now.

If you survived the Year of the Three Funerals, you can survive the Year of Johnny, too.

Still, Cheryl wished fervently that Johnny hadn't tipped his snowmobile. She wished he were going back South of 60° to play hockey and not staying in Iqaluit. Her heart would heal faster if he were gone.

If he were gone she wouldn't do stupid things like neck with Minik in the back seat of a car. She'd done it to punish Johnny for crashing his snowmobile and making her heart jump into her throat with fear. Minik had kissed her back with enthusiasm, and she had felt ugly for using him. Dating him had been a mistake. When Minik asked her out the week after she and Johnny broke up, she'd said yes because that was what she would have said if he'd asked before Johnny moved into town. She'd known Minik for years and liked him; he was unfailingly good-natured and friendly.

She really should break up with him. She would have already if Minik had any deep feelings for her, but, despite his enthusiasm for making out, Cheryl knew her primary attraction for Minik was the fact that she wasn't his cousin. He came from a large family and was related to most of the girls in town who were his age.

The house was dark when she reached it, but her aunt had left the door unlocked for her. The dogs on the porch stirred when Cheryl stepped around them, but recognized her scent and settled back to sleep. Cheryl bent briefly to pat the head of the lead sled dog, Shadow, then silently went inside.

She wasn't sleepy and stayed up for an hour curled up in the living room chair, struggling to get the lines of a poem right. She wrote by the light of a candle so that she wouldn't wake her grandfather, who slept a few feet away on a foldout couch. *Raven wings cut the sky/ Carving a window into night.* She was still up at two in the morning when the phone rang.

Cheryl picked it up right away so her aunt wouldn't get up. She knew even before she said hello who it would be.

When she'd returned from her three-day jaunt on the tundra after she and Johnny broke up, her aunt had complained about a caller who would ring and then hang up, ring and then hang up, over and over. Her aunt had been quite irritated, and, when the phone rang, she'd made Cheryl answer it.

The caller had hung up after Cheryl said hello, but she'd heard the relieved sigh on the other end of the line and known that it was Johnny, that her three-day absence had worried him, and he was checking up on her.

Since then he'd called three times. He never spoke to her, but Cheryl had taken to talking to him. Telling him about her day, about a bird she had seen, winging across the sky that had made her think of her dead baby sister, and how in the old tales dead souls lived for a time in animal bodies before being reborn human. She found it comforting to talk into the silence on the other end of the telephone.

"Hello?" Cheryl spoke softly, so as not to disturb her grandfather's sleep.

Silence. Her aunt would have thought it creepy, but it wasn't. The silence wasn't sly and crafty; it was warm and listening.

Cheryl settled herself more comfortably in her chair and started to talk. She had intended to talk about how her grandfather's arthritis was getting so bad he could hardly bear the cold to train the sled teams and how Aunt Wanda wanted him to sell all the dogs, but the words she heard coming out of her mouth were quite different:

"I saw The Stranger today. I lied when I told Kathy I hadn't." The lie had been instinctive—some things were bad magic, and it was best not to mention them out loud, for fear of attracting their attention by saying their name. Her heart beat quicker even now.

In their late-night conversations Cheryl had taken care never to call him Johnny, or ask him questions. She had been afraid of scaring him off. But tonight Cheryl broke her own rule. The Stranger's appearance on the hill had disturbed her more than she had let herself admit.

"I know you saw him, too." She had seen the fear in his eyes behind the puzzled frown he'd put on for Kathy's benefit.

"It wasn't the first time I saw him either. I saw him the day we met the polar bear." The day before Johnny had broken up with her.

"Who is he, Johnny? Why does he watch you?"

Cheryl held her breath, gripping the phone tight. She was sure Johnny would hang up, but he didn't. She could hear his ghostly breathing over the phone line, rapid and light.

Two seconds. Three. Four. Five. Six seconds.

He wasn't going to answer.

And then he did. "Do you trust me?" Johnny asked.

"No." Cheryl's answer was brutal, truthful. She'd trusted him once, but not anymore. "You're like the Fox, Johnny, a trickster. How can I trust a trickster?"

"You can't," Johnny said and hung up so softly she barely heard the click.

❄ ❄ ❄ ❄

Johnny stood with his head bowed for a long moment after hanging up. He never should have spoken. He'd known his late-night calls to Cheryl were not a good idea, but listening to her low voice had been like a balm. He'd ached to hear about her day, what made her laugh, what made her sad. And he'd thought as long as he didn't say anything he would be safe.

She'd broken the rules first. Saying his name. Mentioning Frost. So he'd taken a chance.

But he'd blown it. And now he could never phone her again.

CHAPTER 5

+5 °C (+41 °F)

THE CAT RAN BETWEEN her legs and outside when Kathy and her dad went out for their morning run. "Sacha, come back," Kathy called, but with little hope. The cat, of course, ignored her.

Sacha had had the run of the base all summer, but Kathy's mom had insisted she become an indoor cat during Iqaluit's harsh winter.

"It's above zero," her dad told her, jogging on the spot. "Leave her."

The run was pleasant, not just for the exercise but because it gave Kathy a chance to spend time with her dad.

"Your Aunt Eloise phoned last night," her dad said, not even slightly out of breath as they ran. He was a fit man in his late forties, his age showing only in his salt and pepper hair. Even relaxing at home, Kathy always had the impression he could spring into action in a microsecond.

"She's all excited because your cousin Marlee won some kind of modelling contest. I told her I wouldn't let any daughter of mine flit off to Paris in the middle of grade twelve, especially with the grades Marlee gets, but she says it's the opportunity of a lifetime."

"She can always take correspondence courses later," Kathy pointed out.

"Yeah, but will she? Marlee's always been one for the easy road," her dad said cynically. "Thank God you're not like that. Ten years from now Marlee will have a photo album; you'll have a career."

Her dad's faith in her gave Kathy a warm glow. He'd always been totally supportive of her ambitions. Her mom supported Kathy, too, but sometimes seemed bewildered by Kathy's unwavering focus on becoming a jet pilot. "I didn't figure out I wanted to be a potter until I was thirty," she'd say.

Kathy's dad was the one who understood her—except sometimes she wondered if he'd noticed she wasn't a boy. He had no concept that she would have loved to be a half as pretty as Marlee.

Kathy had mostly come to terms with her body type. Long legs and a flat chest worked for her in athletics, but she'd also inherited her dad's blade of a nose and bony chin. Her mom was always nagging her to get a stylish short haircut, but Kathy kept resisting. She wasn't giving up her long hair, even if she mostly just shoved in back into a ponytail—it was the one thing that marked her as a girl.

Kathy finished her training run, said goodbye to her dad, and was about to turn into her house when a snowball came out of nowhere and smacked her between the shoulderblades.

"Hey!" She spun around, but couldn't spot the culprit.

None of the soldiers stationed on base would be brave enough to chuck a snowball at Major O'Dwyer's daughter. Which meant... "Johnny?"

When Kathy looked closer, she saw that the snow on her lawn had been tramped down to make a arrow pointing to a set of footprints.

Smiling, Kathy followed the trail, taking bigger strides so that she stepped in the same footprints. The track led around the south wall of the house, zigzagged, made two-footed leaps and ended in a perfect snow angel. She still couldn't see Johnny.

She halted for a moment, baffled, and a snowball hit her, thump, between the shoulder blades.

She whirled around and received a snowball in the face. Before her vision cleared, she gathered up a slushy handful of snow, packed it into a ball and returned the shot. She missed by a mile while Johnny scored two more hits on her shoulders and legs. The cheater had stockpiled a dozen snowballs.

Kathy threw snowballs hard and fast, only missing Johnny once. She ran forward a few steps before exchanging another flurry of snowballs, scoring another three hits.

The fight ended when Johnny swooped forward and slung her over his shoulder like a sack of potatoes. She pounded on his back yelling, "Put me down!" in between giggles.

Johnny slowed to a stop. "You really want me to put you down?"

"Yes!"

"You're sure?"

"Y—yes," Kathy hiccuped. She could feel all the blood going to her head from hanging upside so long.

"Okay." Johnny dropped her in a snowbank.

When he offered her a hand up, Kathy tugged him into the snow, too.

They tussled for a few minutes before Kathy said, "I wasn't expecting you this early." It was only 8:30 a.m. Thanksgiving supper wouldn't be served until 6 p.m. Her dad was working today to give his lieutenant a holiday.

"Yeah, I think the gate guard woke your mom when he phoned to see if he should let me in," Johnny said.

Kathy giggled. "We better stay out of her way a bit longer then." Her poor mom. Her dad insisted the family breakfast together at 6:30 every morning. Kathy knew her mom crawled back into bed as soon as Kathy and her dad went out the door for their morning run.

"Okay," Johnny said. "So what do you want to do now? Oh, wait, I forgot who I was talking to. Does Kathy want to go watch the planes?"

She nodded emphatically.

"Then let's go watch the planes."

Kathy hesitated. "You don't have to. I mean, I can watch them any time. We can go inside and play computer games or something."

Johnny looked amused. "You come to all my hockey games, don't you? I can watch a few planes take off and land. It'll be hard, of course—a grueling ordeal—but I'll bear up. Somehow." He assumed a long-suffering expression.

Kathy punched his arm, and the two of them jogged to the airfield, breaking into a race at the end. Johnny beat her handily.

He stood there, hands on his hips, and shook his head. "That is one huge runway. Kind of overkill, isn't it?"

Kathy laughed. "It's a leftover from the Cold War. The U.S. stationed forces here in case the Soviet Union launched an attack over the pole. They left in the 1960s, and we took over." The base had actually closed for awhile in the 1990s, but had reopened two years ago in the more apprehensive post/911 political climate when it became important to defend Canada's borders from internal terrorist threats as well as external ones.

The town of Iqaluit saw a fair amount of international traffic—planes that stopped to refuel before crossing the ocean. Right now there were two jumbo jets parked in front of the bright yellow commercial airport.

There wasn't much activity on the adjacent military field that day because of the holiday. Kathy was disappointed. Nothing raised her spirits like seeing a fighter jet launch itself, screaming, into the blue sky.

Someday, she promised herself. Someday it's going to be me in the cockpit, breaking Mach I, the speed of sound.

"I can see the appeal of flying," Johnny said, "but why fighter jets? Why not an ultralight or something you could own yourself?"

Kathy scoffed. "Those little toys? It's like driving a minivan instead of a Ferrari."

"Yeah, okay, the speed thing, but—no offense, Kathy—I just can't see you in a war zone."

Johnny had put his finger on her worst fear.

She'd grown up on military bases. Even before 9/11 she'd never had the comfortable illusion of safety most of her peers did. Her father had gone on peace-keeping missions. He'd been injured. She believed that Canada needed a military to protect its freedoms and that just because a job was dirty didn't mean it didn't need doing.

But she was afraid. Afraid that if it came down to the real thing—providing air cover for ground troops while being shot at by anti-aircraft missiles and enemy planes—that she wouldn't be able to hack it. That she wouldn't have the courage to put her duty to her country ahead of her personal safety.

The fear made her angry, and she spoke more sharply than she'd intended, "You're wrong. I'll be fine."

Johnny, always one to avoid confrontation, changed the subject. "So what kind of planes are those?" He pointed to a row of cloud-camouflaged planes.

"CF-18 Hornets," Kathy said, with something like relief.

In response to Johnny's questions, Kathy happily explained that the small symbol on its tail fin meant it belonged to Squadron 437, the Huskies, and that the darker paint job near the front fuselage was supposed to look like a dummy pilot's canopy once the wheels were retracted so as to confuse the enemy during air combat. "You know, so they think it's upside down."

Johnny's next question startled her. "Do you trust me?"

"What?" Kathy tore her gaze from the planes long enough to discover a brooding look on Johnny's usually laughing face.

"Do you trust me?"

"With my life!" She flung out an arm theatrically, but Johnny didn't laugh.

"No, I'm serious, Kathy. Do you trust me? Would you believe me if I told you something really incredible, something you knew couldn't be true?"

Kathy sobered, too, seriously considering his words. Trust Johnny, the world's biggest tease? She'd have to be nuts!

She realized Johnny was taking her silence the wrong way and reached for his hand. "I don't know. You make it kind of hard. You have such a good poker face I can't tell when you're serious or when you're going to say *sucker*."

"So what you're saying is that you trust me only when you know I'm not lying." Johnny kept his face expressionless, but Kathy knew her answer had hurt him.

"No!" She squeezed both of his hands and made him look at her. "That's not what I meant. I may not believe your every word, but I'd trust you with my life."

❀ ❀ ❀ ❀

Kathy trusted him more than Cheryl did. The knowledge lodged uncomfortably in Johnny's stomach—though God knew Cheryl had reason to doubt him.

It didn't matter, Johnny told himself. This was his chance.

Last night Johnny had almost told Cheryl about Frost. He'd never even considered telling anyone before—he'd assumed no one would believe him—and the near miss had awoken an odd hunger inside him. If even just one other person knew about Frost, if Johnny had just one person he could talk to, his burden would be more bearable.

Kathy had seen Frost. She might believe him. Johnny opened his mouth.

You're not thinking to betray me, are you, Johnny? Frost's hated, cold voice was back. Johnny looked up to see Frost standing five feet away behind Kathy's shoulder.

He'd missed his chance.

"Johnny?"

He became aware that Kathy was still looking at him expectantly. "Thank you." He kissed her with cold lips. He really was thankful for her trust. Too bad he'd have to teach her better. A moment later he raised his head, "Kathy?"

"Yes?"

Johnny made himself grin as he stuffed a handful of wet snow down her back. "Sucker."

She shrieked and flung snow in his hair. The battle was back on, but Johnny's heart felt heavy, and he was glad when Kathy called a truce. "Stop. I'm freezing. Let's jog back to the house and go inside."

They jogged two blocks, then turned onto her street. Johnny's step slowed. Frost was there again, standing off to the side in the snow but making no tracks. His black eyes looked like burnt holes.

Johnny looked quickly at Kathy, but she didn't seem to have seen Frost. Yet.

A warning, Johnny.

Johnny saw that Frost was holding something small and black in his arms. A cat. Kathy's cat that was always walking on her textbook and demanding to be petted when they did homework together. Sacha.

The cat struggled silently against being held, clawing and biting. It raked Frost's hands and face, but the scratches on his skin stayed white and did not bleed, and Frost showed no pain. At a touch from him, Sacha stopped fighting, going stiff with fright. Johnny could sense rage in the cat's yellow eyes, but Frost's touch kept it immobile.

As Johnny watched, Frost stroked the cat from head to tail. Frost's hands were ugly, ivory-white with long black fingernails and only four fingers. Under his hand, the cat's black fur turned white, frosted over. He touched the cat's ears and the tips broke off.

Enough, Johnny wanted to scream. *Stop it!* But all he could do was put his arm around Kathy's shoulder to snuggle her closer and spare her the sight.

Thin white lips smiled cruelly as Frost put his hand on Sacha's tail and pinched. The top half of the cat's tail went limp and frozen. Dead.

Johnny looked away. When he turned back Frost had vanished, apparently satisfied that Johnny knew his place again. The cat was a small huddle of black on the snow.

"Hey, Kathy," Johnny said. His voice came out raw and hoarse, not casual at all. "Isn't that your cat?"

CHAPTER 6

-0 °C (+32 °F)

KATHY LET OUT A LOW CRY of dismay when she got a closer look at her cat. Sacha's once-proud black coat looked matted and dull, stiff with ice. The top half of her tail hung limply, and the tips of her ears had frozen off.

Yellow eyes stared up at Kathy, and the cat meowed accusingly.

Johnny came up behind her. "Oh, no."

"She's frozen." Tears pricked Kathy's eyes. She should have put Sacha back inside when she went for her run. Those frozen ears looked horrible. And her tail! It looked broken.

"Let's get her inside." Johnny tried to scoop Sacha up, but the cat arched her back and hissed.

Kathy was startled. Sacha was normally a very friendly cat and often curled up in Johnny's lap when they were watching TV. "She must be scared. Let me try. She knows me better."

Johnny didn't listen. He picked up the squirming cat, stuffing her inside his jacket, close to his body heat. "Poor kitty," he crooned, ignoring the scratches she was giving him. "Had a little run in with Jack Frost, didn't you?" There was something a little strange about his voice, but Kathy was too upset to try to figure out what.

While Johnny stood in the porch holding Sacha, Kathy kicked off her boots and called her mother. "Mom, come quick! Sacha's hurt."

Her mom must have been working at her potter's wheel because when she came into the kitchen she was wearing a ratty pink T-shirt bedaubed with clay. Her auburn hair stuck out all over, and her glasses were smudged. "What is it?"

Kathy gestured, throat too tight to speak.

One look was enough for her mom to understand and take charge. "Kathy, call the vet." She took Sacha from Johnny and cat went from hisses to pitiful mewling.

Kathy dialled the vet clinic, but the torrent of words she poured out when the phone was picked up was met only by the answering machine. "They're closed for the holiday," Kathy reported back to her mom. "What are we going to do?"

"The first thing to do is get Sacha warm," her mom said briskly. "Let's move her into the kitchen. Kathy, turn on the oven and open the oven door so the room heats up faster. Johnny, run down the hall. There should be a load of hot towels just finishing up in the dryer."

Kathy obeyed gladly. Her mom might look artsy-craftsy, but she was very good in an emergency. Just having her there calmed Kathy down.

Johnny, too, was eager to help, bounding down the hall and returning with towels overflowing his arms.

Her mom picked one out and, gently, wrapped the cat in it, forming a nest with only Sacha's head peeking out.

"Won't the ice melt into her fur and make her colder?" Kathy asked anxiously.

"You're right," her mom said. "Go get a comb. We'll try to brush it out."

Sacha didn't like the comb. Kathy had to hold the cat firmly, while her mom used the comb to pick ice particles out of her fur. It was a tedious process. They sent Johnny for warm towels twice more, but when they were done Sacha had stopped shivering and even began to purr. The top half of her tail might still fall off, but Sacha would live.

Once the crisis was past, Kathy suddenly remembered Johnny's scratches. She insisted that he wash them. While he was putting on antibacterial cream, her mom asked, "What happened?"

Guilt choked Kathy; she started to cry. "She got out when Dad and I went outside this morning. I should have let her back in before we went down to the airfield, but I didn't think of it. It didn't seem that cold." The temperature had to have been above zero, or the snowballs wouldn't have packed so well. Had it dropped while they watched the planes?

Johnny squeezed her shoulders. "It wasn't your fault."

Kathy couldn't bear to be too far away from Sacha, so they stayed inside for the rest of the day, playing Monopoly, and later helping her mom make supper.

Kathy made the salad. Her mother liked to throw everything in the fridge in, and Kathy was a firm believer that deviled eggs did not belong in a salad. Her mom set Johnny to work peeling potatoes. He wasn't very practiced at it and kept getting peelings on the floor instead of in the garbage. One hit Kathy's arm. "Oops," Johnny said, too innocently.

His next flicks hit her knee and her shoe, and she realized he could aim them as deftly as a hockey puck. "Hey!" The next one hit her chin, and her mom started laughing.

Johnny had just managed to get a potato peeling on the ceiling when her dad came home from work at four and found them in the kitchen.

Kathy tried not to look up at the potato peeling still clinging to the ceiling.

Her dad was looking at Johnny with a disapproving frown.

Uh-oh.

Johnny had initially made a good impression on her dad, who had scared off more than one potential boyfriend of hers. When she'd introduced him Johnny had shaken his hand, looked him square in the eye and told him he'd have Kathy home on time, safe and sound. Volunteering to help do yard work hadn't hurt either.

But when Kathy told her dad about the snowmobile accident, he'd been pretty tight-lipped. "So I hear you had an accident yesterday."

"Yeah."

The potato peeling fell, and her dad picked it up. "I talked to your uncle, and he said the snowmobile was completely wrecked."

Another bad sign. He'd phoned Johnny's uncle.

"It was entirely my fault," Johnny said.

Her dad frowned. "Why? Were you being reckless?"

"I should have known the hill was too steep. I'm just thankful Kathy wasn't hurt."

Kathy jumped in. "I wasn't hurt because you rolled me out of the way."

But Johnny wouldn't take credit for saving her. "I should have made Kathy get off before I attempted the hill."

"So why didn't you?"

This was beginning to sound like the third degree. *Do something,* Kathy mouthed at her mom.

Her mom cleared her throat. "Speaking of accidents, Sacha had a misadventure this afternoon." She told her husband about the cat's frozen ears and tail. "From now on, Sacha stays inside."

"But it's barely zero out there," her dad protested, baffled.

"It wasn't an accident."

Everyone turned to look at Johnny.

"Remember the ice in her fur? I think someone deliberately got her wet so she'd freeze."

Kathy and her mom both stared at him, appalled. "Who would do such a horrible thing?" her mom asked.

Johnny shrugged, but his jaw was tight with anger.

Kathy was mortified when her dad fixed Johnny with an eagle-eyed stare. "Do you know who did it?"

Johnny went very still. "If you're asking me if I did it, the answer is no."

"Dad!" Kathy protested. "Johnny was with me the entire time." Except, she suddenly remembered, for their brief game of hide and seek. Not that it mattered. Johnny was incapable of such a cruel act.

Her dad ignored her. "Do you have any idea why anyone would do such a thing?"

"Maybe it was a warning." Johnny met and held her dad's gaze, unflinching.

"The power's out," Kathy's mom said.

Neither her dad nor Johnny seemed to hear, focused on their own conversation.

"A warning for what?" Her dad's interest sharpened. "Have you heard rumours about some group protesting? Is someone upset about the reopening of Iqaluit airbase?" There had been a few acts of vandalism in the last town they'd lived in, but Kathy hadn't had any hint of anti-military feeling here.

Johnny shrugged.

"I said, the power just went out," her mom repeated more loudly.

Kathy looked up. It was still light outside, so she hadn't noticed the kitchen light fixture going off, but the furnace had shut off, too, and, of course, the oven light. "The turkey." She and her mom exchanged chagrined looks.

"Maybe it will come back on by itself in a few minutes," her mom said, ever the optimist.

It didn't.

The airbase had its own generator, but her dad investigated and found out that the problem was exclusive to their own house, an electrical problem. Someone came to take a look at it, but had a frustrating time tracking down the source. The power remained off. The turkey was ruined, the stuffing was ruined, the potatoes were raw.

"Sorry about this," Kathy said miserably. Johnny looked grim. "You still have time to go home and eat Thanksgiving there."

"I could call my aunt and uncle," Johnny volunteered. "They probably have turkey enough to feed us all."

Kathy's mom rallied. "No, it's almost five thirty—way too late to spring a surprise like that on her. We'll just have to make some substitutions," she said, determinedly cheerful. "We can have take-out fried chicken instead of turkey, and fries instead of mashed potatoes."

Kathy tried to be positive. "The salad should still be okay, and I could go next door and ask to use their microwave to warm up the corn. And the pumpkin pie is ready, too."

It was a strange meal, served by candlelight, but not bad.

"It feels more like Halloween than Thanksgiving," Kathy joked when they'd abandoned the dishes and adjourned to the darkened living room. "We should tell ghost stories." She waved her candle for effect.

Her mom jumped on the idea with enthusiasm, making up a story about a haunted house. Kathy retold her favourite, "The Legend of Sleepy Hollow", embroidering over the bits she didn't remember very well. Even her dad got in the spirit, telling a "true story" about a lost spy plane that had gone down in a storm in the Arctic during the Cold War and supposedly had a nuclear missile on board.

Johnny demurred when his turn came. "I'm no good at scary stories."

At 9:30 the gate guard called to say that Evan had arrived to pick Johnny up and asked permission to let him through. Kathy walked Johnny to the door. Her mom winked and steered her dad away, giving them a moment of privacy.

Instead of kissing him, Kathy looked at him, troubled. She couldn't get Sacha out of her mind. "Do you really think some nut tried to kill our cat?"

Johnny put on his jacket, not looking at her. "If you want to blame someone, blame Jack Frost."

Kathy blinked. "What?"

"You know, Jack Frost." Johnny smiled, his voice playful, but something was a little off about his expression, as if he didn't really think the subject was amusing. "The little man who draws patterns on the windows at night. Didn't your mother ever tell you about him?"

"Yes, but—"

"Did you believe it?"

Kathy frowned, perplexed. "At the time. Like the tooth fairy."

"Ah, but there is a tooth fairy. Your parents take the tooth and replace it with a quarter. If you stayed up long enough, you could catch the tooth fairy." Johnny paused. "Did you?"

Kathy was confused. "Did I what?"

"Did you catch the tooth fairy?"

"No." She smiled faintly. "I forgot to tell Mom I was putting a tooth under my pillow one night, and the tooth fairy didn't come." She still had the tooth, but she didn't tell Johnny that.

"I did."

"What?"

"I caught the tooth fairy," Johnny repeated patiently. "And Santa Claus. And the Easter Bunny. Then I'd tell Evan that they weren't real. I was a brat," Johnny said without inflection. "When Mom told Evan about Jack Frost, I said I'd catch him too. Mom just laughed. She said no one could catch Jack Frost." Another pause.

"So you stayed up that night?" Kathy prompted. She had the strange feeling Johnny was trying to tell her something, but she didn't understand what.

"So I stayed up that night," Johnny agreed, face expressionless. "And I caught him—Jack Frost. Or rather he caught me."

Kathy frowned. Because of course there was no Jack Frost. The crystallization of water caused the pretty patterns on the windowpane. That was all. No little man with sharp carving tools. No Jack Frost.

Then the light dawned. "Oh, I get it. You're telling a ghost story. That's a pretty good one." She punched his arm lightly. "You had me going for a moment there."

Johnny smiled, a bleak, wintry smile. "Are you saying you don't believe me?" His voice turned silky. "I thought you said you trusted me, Kathy."

She stared. He was just teasing, wasn't he? "I can't win," she complained. "If I say no, I don't trust you. If I say yes, I'm a sucker."

Johnny's expression changed again. "Poor Kathy." He chucked her under the chin. "I don't play fair, do I?" He didn't wait for her answer, just went out the door, coat still unbuttoned.

❄ ❄ ❄ ❄

Johnny wished Frost was just a ghost story or a little man who made patterns on windows. But Frost was more. Johnny suspected that Frost was an old god, one worshipped so long ago that only fragments of tales about him still remained. Little pieces that hinted nothing of the whole.

Frost was Cold and Nothing and Void. Johnny had seen his power. Kathy had only felt it brush by her today.

Frost's restraint disturbed Johnny. He'd started telling his little story as a test to see if Frost was always listening, figuring he'd stop as soon as Frost said anything. Frost's usual pattern would be to demand that Johnny break up with Kathy, and Johnny had decided he was willing to take that risk.

Frost had let Johnny get farther into his story than Johnny had thought he would, before saying, *Enough*. Johnny had obediently stopped. Frost, Johnny thought bitterly, had him well-trained.

But then Frost had left without demanding that he break up with Kathy. Without punishing Johnny. Now that he thought about it, Frost's attack on Kathy's cat seemed out of character, too. Frost was usually very... direct with his threats.

Did Frost want Johnny to date Kathy? Why? Johnny could only come up with one explanation: Frost wanted him to have access to the airbase.

CHAPTER 7

-20 °C (-4 °F)

THE FIRST ANNIVERSARY was always the worst.

November 3. Today Cheryl's father had been dead for five years.

There had been tears in Grandfather's eyes when he'd patted her arm this morning. Sometimes she forgot that her father had also been his son. Aunt Wanda's brother.

Cheryl almost hadn't gone to school, but she'd bullied herself into it. *It's been five years. How long are you going to keep running to the hills when the anniversaries come up? Ten years? Twenty? Thirty? Will the ache have eased by then?*

It will never ease. So you might as well go to school.

So she'd gone and was now regretting it. She sat with the rest of the group at lunch hour, silent, unamused by Johnny's antics.

There is a stone in my heart/
dragging me down/
to the bottom of the sea.

All the poetry inside her that day was dark.

Cheryl looked at her watch. 12:30. Eleven and a half hours left in this miserable day. Then a month's respite, then the second anniversary, December 5, and the third anniversary, December 8.

She felt hollow inside, but couldn't eat.

She looked up once and caught Johnny watching her. He immediately glanced away, but a moment later he said to the group, "Let's all skip class this afternoon. Go out on the ice. I'm tired of being cooped up inside for all the daylight hours."

"I can't," Kathy said. "I have a test."

"Me, too," Tracy sighed. "One more bad mark in math, and I'm toast."

"Ditto," Evan said. Kathy, Tracy and Evan were all in grade eleven and shared most of the same classes. "You shouldn't go either," Evan told his brother. "Uncle Dan said he might let you play junior hockey in January if you buckled down and got better marks."

Johnny scoffed. "That's in January. It's November now."

"And you have mid-terms in two weeks," Evan murmured.

Johnny ignored him. "Minik, how about you?"

"Can't. I promised my cousin I'd help him work on his snowmobile this afternoon." Minik grinned.

"Brendan?"

Brendan held up his hands. "Count me out. I know everyone says the sea is frozen over solid until next summer, but I don't feel safe on it. I keep remembering that story Minik told us about some guy getting trapped on a piece of pack ice and floating out to sea. And then discovering he was sharing the ice with a polar bear. No thank you."

Johnny turned to Cheryl, grinning. "Looks like it's just you and me."

Cheryl's heart turned over. She had the sudden suspicion that Johnny had known exactly what the response to his suggestion to cut class would be. He must have known Evan, Tracy and Kathy had a math test, Brendan had refused to go out on the sea ice before, and Minik might have told him about the engine he planned to overhaul.

She shouldn't go with him. But Cheryl didn't think she could stand being closed up in the school for one more minute. "I'll get my coat."

Cheryl saw alarm flare in Kathy's eyes at the prospect of Johnny going off with his old girlfriend. Saw her open her mouth and then close it again. Math tests would always be more important to Kathy than Johnny was.

❄ ❄ ❄ ❄

Ice. Ice everywhere, all around her. Cheryl turned in a circle and could make out the smudge of chimney smoke from Iqaluit a mile away, kept turning and saw only ice. Sea ice was not smooth like a skating rink, but rough and bumpy, full of small hummocks and valleys. It was not white either. Every dip and indentation had its own blue shadow which would turn purplish when the sun set a little after three. And the ice itself was dirty and discoloured in places, yellowish.

Cheryl loved it.

Some people hated winter. Cheryl's mother had been one of those people. She hadn't been able to see that winter balanced summer; she had wanted it to be summer all year long. If you didn't like winter you had no business living North of 60°, in Cheryl's opinion.

It was cold, -20 °C plus wind-chill, but she felt exhilarated. She stamped her feet to keep her toes warm inside her kamik boots and kept her face out of the wind, but that was all.

She stood there for a long time in silence, letting the wind blow all her troubles away. Her soul felt cleansed when she finished.

She turned to Johnny, who had been standing silently about five feet away the whole time. "Thank you."

Cheryl knew silence was not easy for Johnny. It was as if he feared that if he stopped talking and joking he would cease to exist. When they first started dating she had shown him the silences of the North, laying her hand across his mouth whenever he started to crack an uneasy joke. "Shh," she had whispered, and finally he had hushed. Listened to the moan of the wind sweeping across the land. Listened to the faint cries of birds, wheeling far overhead.

He had gripped her hand tight as if falling off the edge of the world.

Now Cheryl held out her hand, and Johnny took it. This time she was the one to squeeze so hard she cut off his circulation. She didn't look at him, staring out at the ice, as she began to talk. She'd told him bits of the story when they'd dated last spring, but not the whole thing.

"My dad was out ice fishing. Another hunter mistook my dad for a caribou. Shot him in the chest. He died instantly. The shooter hadn't been drinking or anything, it was just an accident, but I hated him for killing my dad." Just thinking about him made black hate boil up inside her. "Why didn't he look more closely? Why didn't he wait?" Cheryl stopped and bit her lip.

Johnny patted her back. He looked uncomfortable with what she was saying, but she didn't care. She had to tell someone. It felt all bottled up inside of her.

"I can still remember the moment when we got the news. Mrs. Klein, our neighbour, came over and woke up my mother, Remy—which was not an easy task, since Remy was drunk. Mrs. Klein spoke in whispers, but Remy cried out, 'Dead? What do you mean dead? He can't be dead.'" Her screaming had woken the baby. Cheryl had picked up her sister and began rocking her automatically, as the news sunk in. Her father was dead.

Mrs. Klein had held Remy, and Cheryl had held the baby, but there had been no one to hold Cheryl.

"Mrs. Klein stayed with us for a couple of days, but left in an offended huff when Remy cursed her out for taking away her bottle."

"Was your mother always an alcoholic?" Johnny asked.

"Pretty much. For as long as I can remember, anyway, but Dad controlled her liquor supply to some extent. We had some happy times." Whatever bitter thoughts Cheryl had about Remy, Cheryl had never doubted one thing: Remy had loved her father. The grief Remy had fallen into after his funeral had been black and total.

"Let me guess," Johnny said roughly. "Your mom went back to her bottle, and you were left alone with the baby."

"Yes. Everyone tried to help us, Mrs. Klein, my mother's cousins, my parent's friends, but Remy kept pushing them away so I did, too. I felt like accepting help was a betrayal of my mother, so after awhile everyone just gave up."

"You were just a kid. You shouldn't have been left alone to deal with that," Johnny said angrily.

"Oh, I found my own solution," Cheryl said bitterly. "Like mother, like daughter."

"You don't drink."

"No. But one afternoon I slipped out while the baby napped. I couldn't stand being in the house a moment longer. I came across a group of older kids in the woods, taking turns sniffing gasoline. One of them noticed that I'd been crying and offered me a turn. She said it would make me feel better. She seemed so... kind." Remy yelled or cried or was occasionally affectionate, bestowing sloppy kisses, but she was never kind. Not when she was drunk. And Remy was always drunk.

"The gasoline fumes made me feel better. A few sniffs and my problems just seemed to float away. I didn't care that my dad was dead and Remy was a drunk. It didn't matter." Cheryl clenched her fists. "I liked that feeling. A lot. I started to sneak out almost every afternoon.

"I was higher than a kite, when I came home one day to find Remy blacked out on the couch, the house stone cold, and the baby sick. Even high, I knew there was something wrong with the baby's cough and the way she cried, so much weaker than her normal screams. I tried to wake Remy, but she just kept snoring. It took me close to an hour to think of going next door to Mrs. Klein for help."

That hour haunted Cheryl. "Ever since then I've always wondered: if I'd been sober and I'd gotten the baby to the hospital right away, would my sister still be alive?"

"You can't think like that." Johnny hugged her close, rocking her. "You were just a kid. You did all you could."

"Maybe." Cheryl was unconvinced. "But all I could wasn't enough. She died of pneumonia in a city hospital three days later." The body had been shipped back for the funeral.

The coffin had been tiny and white.

"The night after the baby's funeral Remy committed suicide."

"God!" Johnny's arms tightened around her. "I suppose you found her body, too."

"No, I was spared that at least. My best friend's mom insisted I stay with them after my sister's funeral, all but locked me in the house. She knew I wouldn't get the comfort I needed at home, but all I could see afterward was that if I'd been home Remy might not have felt so alone. Might not have..." Cheryl cleared her clogged throat. "It wasn't true. Remy would have found a way to do it anyhow, but I said some terrible things to Susan's mom..." Things she bitterly regretted. After moving away, she'd apologized by letter, but the words had seemed so terribly stilted and the reply she'd gotten even more so.

"Two days later I got to attend my third funeral of the year. That one was almost painless because I got high again. I felt like I was watching a TV show from a mountaintop. I could see everything, but it didn't seem to have anything to do with me."

"What happened?"

"Grandfather came." She'd barely understood what was happening when her grandfather, whom she'd only seen twice before, once at her father's funeral, came to take her away. He'd spent two months with her out on the land, far away from towns and gasoline. He'd never once rebuked her for her tantrums and screaming fits, just gently, over and over, showed her the traditional Inuit way of life and taught her to speak Inuktitut. The dogs had reached her first, friendly and impossible to rebuff. Soon she'd been playing with them, and it had been natural to ask her grandfather how to feed and care for them.

Her years with her mother had taught her not to trust, but Grandfather's gentleness had stolen under her defences. Slowly, without Cheryl ever being conscious of making the decision, she'd come to trust him.

"Grandfather saved me." Cheryl raised her head and looked up at Johnny. "What about you? What's your story?"

Johnny shrugged. "I don't have one."

"Tell me about your parents." Johnny never talked about them. Cheryl knew they had died in a car accident about ten years before—Evan had mentioned it once—but none of the details.

He began to look uneasy. "Nothing to tell, really." He changed the subject quite deliberately. "You know, standing out here it's easy to imagine that we're living in an ice age."

"Tell me about your parents, Johnny."

"Did you know we're living in an ice epoch?" Johnny chatted. "I did an oral report on it once. Hey, I bet I still have my speech memorized." Johnny began speaking in a TV announcer-type voice. "'Over 10% of the Earth's landmass is covered by ice. A drop of only 10 degrees in the average global temperature could plunge us into the next ice age—'"

"How did they die, Johnny?"

Johnny ignored her, speaking faster and faster, as if once he'd started he couldn't stop until he reached the end. "'...what we think of as normal global temperatures are really only a break between ice ages. The current Holocene interglacial has already lasted 10,000 years and some scientists think is due to end shortly. Everybody thinks global warming will stop it, but there's new research that says global warming may actually speed up the next ice age by shutting off the Gulf Stream that keeps Europe warm. Or we could touch off a nuclear winter ourselves.'"

Johnny was trying to distract her so he wouldn't have to answer her question. Cheryl felt angry and bruised like she'd bounced off a wall. This happened every time she started to feel close to Johnny.

"'During the peak of the last ice age the Laurentide ice sheet covered almost all of Canada. The Barnes or Penny Ice Cap here on Baffin Island may well be the last remnant of it.'"

Cheryl socked his arm—and not gently. He finally stopped.

"I just spilled my guts to you," Cheryl gritted. "Would it be so hard to reciprocate even a little?"

He wouldn't look at her. "Yes, it would, actually."

Despair filled her. He never opened himself up to anyone more than a crack, but because Johnny's exterior shell was so much fun most people never noticed.

Evan felt the lack of closeness and was hurt by it.

Poor Kathy hadn't a clue.

"Do you know why we broke up, Johnny?" Cheryl asked.

"Because we're too different. It was a clash of cultures," Johnny said wearily.

"No." Cheryl shook her head. "That was just the excuse you gave me. The real reason was the polar bear."

Johnny went very still. "What do you mean?"

It had been September then, and the seas had been mostly free of ice, trapping the polar bears on land. While out hiking, Cheryl and Johnny had stumbled upon a polar bear.

It had been an unpleasant surprise for both sides. Cheryl and Johnny had approached upwind from the bear, and a curve in the stream bed they were following had hidden them from view. When the stream emptied out onto the beach, the polar bear had suddenly been right there in front of them.

Even then they might have been okay, but the polar bear had been eating, its white muzzle stained with seal blood, and it moved to defend its food.

The giant bear was easily eight feet long, one thousand pounds of brute power and force. It walked quickly towards them, head down and swinging from side to side. It hissed at them, and rose up on its hind legs so that it towered over them, brandishing its claws.

Cheryl knew enough not to run. She slowly backed up, heart hammering, as the polar bear approached. Cheryl had eaten polar bear, but never before seen a live one up close. The size of the bear made her feel faint and sick. They had no gun, not even a knife.

Johnny stood his ground. Cheryl was horrified when she realized Johnny hadn't moved with her. He stood there, dwarfed by the polar bear and said, "You win. Just don't kill her."

The polar bear gnashed its teeth and swiped at the air in front of Johnny. Its claws came within inches of his face.

"You've got me. *Just leave her alone.*"

The polar bear went back down on four legs and returned to its meal as if it had never been disturbed.

Cheryl backed up on shaky legs. She was watching the bear in case it changed its mind, but she noticed that Johnny was looking slightly off to the side. She followed his gaze and saw The Stranger for the first time. He was only there for a moment, but it was long enough for Cheryl to sense that there was something wrong about his face, his dark eyes, and to feel menace coming off him in waves. She yanked her gaze away before he saw her watching him and, for reasons she could never explain to herself afterward, carefully pretended that she'd never seen him at all.

"We did *not* break up because of a polar bear," Johnny said, bringing her out of the memory. "That's ridiculous." His voice was scoffing, but Cheryl saw a hint of fear in his eyes.

"The polar bear could have killed either of us that day," Cheryl said. "It frightened you."

"Of course, it did. Who wouldn't be scared?" Johnny asked.

Cheryl lifted her chin. "It frightened you, because it made you realize just how much you cared for me." The wind rose to a scream, trying to stuff the words back down her throat, but Cheryl would not stop. "And caring is dangerous, isn't it, Johnny? You and I both know that. Three funerals for me, two for you. If you care, if you trust someone, you might get hurt. And that's why you broke up with me the next day."

Johnny's mask slipped just a little; she saw torment in his eyes. "Maybe," he said. "Maybe that's true, but it doesn't change anything—"

Suddenly, the ice cracked with a sound like a gunshot, and sea water washed over the toe of Cheryl's kamik.

Instinctively, Cheryl took a step back, and the crack widened, black water showing between her and Johnny. Between her and land. She was on an iceberg.

"No!" Johnny looked horrified. Instead of retreating from the dangerous lip, he edged forward, holding out his hand. "Hurry! Take my hand! Jump!"

Cheryl balked. The sea ice was miles long; chances were that the piece of ice she was on was still connected to the mainland farther up. While she hesitated, the rift was widening with every second, now six inches across, then eight.

"Now, Cheryl!" Desperation greyed Johnny's face. He inched closer to the edge, and water licked at his boots.

It was over a foot across now. She wouldn't be able to make it. "No, stay back! I'll find another way across," Cheryl yelled. If he fell in the water, he would slip underneath the ice and never find his way back up.

Johnny took a few steps back and Cheryl's heart lightened—*he'd listened*—and then he ran forward at the crack. Leaped the two-foot gap. He landed on his knees, and his impact made the ice dip under slightly. Water soaked his jeans to the knees.

"Johnny!" Cheryl pulled him up, pulled him away from the edge. Her heart was in her throat, she'd been so afraid that he would die, that anger boiled up in her for putting her through it. "Well, that was brilliant," she snapped at him. "Now we might both be trapped. Who's going to get the rescuers now?"

Johnny wasn't listening. "Come on, hurry." He started to lead her away from the fissure, but angling back toward the bay.

It almost worked.

Then another crack appeared five feet in front of them, snaking through the ice like lightning. The ice popped and groaned ominously.

Cheryl slowed; Johnny didn't. He yanked her forward. For a moment, Cheryl thought he just hadn't seen the crack. "Stop!" She pulled on his arm.

"Jump!" he yelled back.

He was still pulling on her, and she was afraid that if she didn't jump her weight would drag him down and they would both go into the sea. She closed her eyes and jumped.

Johnny jumped farther than she; her shoulder got wrenched, and she landed awkwardly on one hand and both knees. She gasped painfully as her kneecap connected with the unforgiving ice. She wanted to just lie there and gasp, but water spread under her gloves. Johnny was pulling at her again. "Come on!"

She staggered up and ran, the nylon of her ski pants swishing annoyingly, hindering her less-than-graceful stride even more. *This shouldn't be happening,* she thought as more cracks appeared ahead of them. *The sea ice has been frozen for weeks, and it's minus twenty today.* But the ice kept cracking under them, breaking up like rotten wood, as if it was summer thaw.

Cheryl ran and jumped and fell what seemed like a dozen times, Johnny's hand manacling her wrist. He never let go, his hold never loosened, even though she was slowing him down, perhaps fatally. She didn't try to argue, just ran and jumped as best as she could, until they finally made it to shore.

Her breath knifed in her lungs. She lay there gasping, trying to gobble down enough oxygen to make the spots dancing in front of her eyes go away. Her limbs felt like seaweed.

The cold penetrated her ski pants, but the beach felt wonderfully solid. It was the thought of Johnny's wet jeans that finally brought her head up. He needed to get inside fast.

Johnny wasn't there.

She sat up, and she saw him farther down the beach, talking to someone, a man too far away for her to see his face.

Johnny!" She called his name, but he never looked back. The other man was gone now, and Johnny just kept walking farther and farther away, shoulders hunched. After a moment, Cheryl gave up. She pounded her fist on the snow-encrusted dune, then got up and trekked back home by herself, her heart a stone in her chest.

❊ ❊ ❊ ❊

Johnny tried to tackle Frost. "You bastard!" he howled.

Johnny made contact, felt his arms go around Frost, felt Frost's start of surprise—and that sure as hell didn't happen very often—but when Johnny hit the ground there was no one under him. Frost had slipped away and was standing a few feet away, looking unamused.

Bastard. Johnny hated him. "If you ever, ever do something like that again... if you ever hurt Cheryl, I'll—" He stopped. There was nothing he could do to hurt Frost, and many, many things Frost could do to hurt him.

"You'll do nothing," Frost said, voice as cold as icicles.

"—I'll move to Florida," Johnny said recklessly on a burst of anger. "Just try to catch me there."

"If you ever try to run, I will freeze your flying machine and cause it to fall into the sea," Frost said after a small pause. Johnny looked intently into Frost's dark eyes; had he flinched just slightly at the mention of Johnny going south?

"As for the girl," Frost continued, "she is merely frightened."

"There was no reason for you to frighten her," Johnny said. "I wasn't going to tell her anything."

"Your conversation was growing perilous."

Johnny looked up in surprise. Cheryl had mentioned meeting the polar bear, yes, but she hadn't mentioned seeing Frost—The Stranger, was what she'd called him on the phone. Frost hadn't intervened that time. Why? Because Johnny had hung up fast enough, or, Johnny's heart started to beat harder, was it because the conversation had taken place on a phone?

Frost was old, millennia old. Phones, especially in this part of the world, hadn't been around that long in comparison. Maybe Frost didn't know how they worked. Maybe he could only hear Johnny's side of the conversation.

For the first time Johnny felt a thread of hope. *He could work around Frost.*

CHAPTER 8

-25 °C (-13 °F)

JOHNNY WAS LOOKING AT CHERYL AGAIN, Kathy noticed, or maybe she was just being paranoid. Cheryl sat two seats ahead of Johnny in the row. Maybe Johnny was just looking at the notes on the whiteboard.

Or maybe, Kathy watched Johnny with a lump of jealousy in her throat, Johnny stared at Cheryl in all his classes and Kathy just didn't know about it because this was the only class she took with them. Ever since the two of them went off together on the ice two weeks ago, Johnny had seemed different, more distant.

Inuksuk High School hadn't been able to afford a separate teacher to teach English 20 this year, so the grade eleven English 20 students had been put into two split classes. Kathy was in the same classroom as Cheryl and Johnny, who were in grade twelve, but Evan was in with the grade ten English class.

Kathy tried to attract Johnny's attention. "So what mark did you get on your assignment? I got an A-." When Johnny turned away from the fascinating view of the back of Cheryl's head, Kathy showed him her creative writing story.

Johnny smiled at her, but he seemed distracted. "I did pretty good actually."

Ms. Lark cleared her throat. "I'd like a couple of you to read your work to the class. Let's see. Johnny, how about you? And Cheryl, too."

Kathy tensed. She didn't like hearing their names paired together even in such an innocent way.

"I don't want to read mine aloud," Cheryl said.

Ms. Lark studied her for a moment, then nodded. "If you're uncomfortable reading it, then—"

"I'll read it for her," Johnny interrupted. "If she'll read my story. I'm too shy to read my own story aloud."

The class laughed at the idea of Johnny being shy. Kathy forced a smile, but under her desk her hands clenched.

"Cheryl?" Ms. Lark asked. "Would that be okay with you?"

Cheryl looked at Johnny. She was serious, not laughing. Neither was Johnny. He looked intense. Kathy's stomach sank. He wanted to read Cheryl's poem, wanted Cheryl to read his story, she realized. Cheryl nodded slowly, her gaze still locked with Johnny's.

The connection between them was palpable, like a live wire, and Kathy felt cold and uneasy.

She was being silly. This must be one of Johnny's gags. He would probably read Cheryl's poem in a squeaky voice and crack the whole class up.

But his voice when he read the poem was rich and serious:

Gasoline

Standing on top of the world,
arms spread wide,
embracing the sky.
Laughing,
knowing I can fly.
Jumping,
finding I cannot.

At first Kathy couldn't figure the poem out. Why was it called Gasoline? Finding she could not what? Jump? Curious, Kathy looked at Cheryl. Something in Cheryl's calm lack of expression struck Kathy as wrong. As if Cheryl was merely pretending not to mind that her poem had been read aloud.

Gasoline. Hadn't Kathy read an article about teenagers who'd gotten high sniffing gasoline?

An image came to Kathy of a girl standing on a rooftop, giggling, so high on gasoline fumes that she believed she was a bird and could fly. She saw the girl jumping—and falling like a stone.

Kathy stared. Was the girl in the poem Cheryl? Had Cheryl once been addicted and stood on a roof?

Kathy's story about the space shuttle making an emergency landing at the designated landing site in Iqaluit because of a hurricane at Cape Canaveral suddenly seemed shallow.

"My turn to read yours." Cheryl held out her hand to Johnny in demand. Silently, Johnny gave her his story, and Kathy once again sensed undercurrents flowing between them.

Cheryl began to read:

Through the Ice

"Aren't we there yet?" the little boy whined, poking his head into the front seat of the car.

"Not yet," his father said grimly, glaring at the boy in the rear view mirror. "Now sit down and play with your brother. I'm trying to—"

"WATCH OUT!" his mother screamed.

A dog bounded across the road.

His father hit the brakes to avoid it, and the car spun like a top on the glare ice. Horizon whirling, the car skidded off the road and onto a pond.

When the car finally stopped everyone was silent for a moment.

"Is everyone all right?" Their mother unhooked her seat belt and started to crawl into the back.

"That was fun," said the little boy. "Can we do it again?"

His younger brother sobbed.

CRACK!

"What the hell—?" his dad started to say.

CRACK, CRACK, CRACK, CRACK!

The noises were as loud as gunfire. The little boy looked out the window and saw a web of cracks forming on the pond ice. Underneath he could see black water.

CRACK!

The back tire broke through first. The car listed briefly to the right before the ice gave way everywhere and the car plunged through.

The windows went black, and cold water poured in through the floorboards, soaking the little boy's socks. He and his brother screamed together. The little boy undid his seat belt and stood on the seat.

"We have to get out!" his mother yelled. She pulled on the door latch.

"No!" His father lunged forward, but proved too late. A black wall of water rushed in, smashing her back against her husband and the steering wheel.

Cold water surged past the little boy's knees then shoulders, numbing his legs, and trying to drag him under. The bubble of air trapped in the car grew smaller and smaller.

The little boy screamed as black water rushed into his nose and mouth, filling them—

Kathy shivered as she listened to Cheryl read. She would never have guessed that reckless Johnny had such a vivid imagination and talent for description.

After class, she went up to Johnny, very conscious that Cheryl was still dawdling nearby.

"That was a good story. If you ever want to give up hockey maybe you can become a writer." Cheryl was still gathering up her books, being really slow. Kathy smiled again, brightly. "But don't you think it would be better to have a happy ending?" Both parents and the brother had survived, but the little boy had drowned.

"Nah," Johnny said. "The little brat caused the accident. He deserved to die."

"Johnny!" Kathy protested his harsh assessment while taking his arm and steering him towards the door. Away from Cheryl.

❀ ❀ ❀ ❀

Had Cheryl heard? Had she understood?

Somebody hear me, Johnny thought. *Somebody, please. Anybody.*

❀ ❀ ❀ ❀

At the next post-game victory party that Saturday Kathy kept close to Johnny's elbow. Cheryl stayed on the opposite side of the room, but the way she and Johnny were avoiding one another only made Kathy surer that there was still something between them.

Yesterday, she would have said that Cheryl was shallow and didn't deserve Johnny, but after hearing Cheryl's poem she didn't have that comforting illusion. Cheryl was more than she'd thought.

Kathy didn't know what to do. She reminded herself that it had been Johnny's choice to break up with Cheryl and start dating Kathy. If he liked Cheryl, all he had to do was break up with Kathy. He'd shown no sign of wanting to do that, so she must be mistaken about his feelings for Cheryl. Right?

On the other hand, Kathy and Johnny's relationship was more affectionate than romantic. And she was almost positive Cheryl was in love with Johnny.

Cheryl had broken up with Minik last week.

And what about her own feelings? Did she love Johnny? Kathy considered the thought. There had been moments when she'd felt almost in love with him, but she didn't think she was truly in love. She liked him a lot, was attracted to him and enjoyed his company. Johnny was fun.

He was also popular. Kathy admitted to herself that she had been flattered to be asked out by the most popular guy in school. It had been a vindication that she was no longer Giraffe.

Popularity was a dumb reason to date anyone.

Kathy came to a decision. "Johnny, I need to talk to you. Alone," she said abruptly, interrupting his story.

"Sure." Johnny smiled easily and slung an arm around her shoulders. "Where do you want to go?" There were only about fifteen people at the party, but music blasted from the stereo system, making it hard to talk.

They ended up grabbing their coats and sitting outside in the car. From the winks they'd gotten, everyone seemed to assume they were going outside to neck, but Kathy kept close to the car door. Not even the spectacular northern lights show could distract her.

"Can I ask you something?"

"So long as the knowledge doesn't put your life in danger," Johnny said flippantly.

Kathy forged on ahead. "Do you like Cheryl?"

The smile evaporated off Johnny's face. "What do you mean?"

This was hard. Kathy breathed in slowly. "In class this week, when you read one another's assignments, I kind of got the feeling that you... cared for her."

"She's a friend." Johnny evaded her eyes, staring out the window at the red and green dancing northern lights. "This far north I feel like the next ice age has already begun."

Kathy ignored his attempt to change the subject. "And what about me? Am I just a friend, too? Who do you like better?"

"Can't I like you both equally?" The window was starting to frost up from their breath, and Johnny pressed his palm to the glass, warming a small peephole.

Kathy continued bravely. "Because if you like Cheryl better maybe we should break up." She held her breath.

Feathery spirals of frost covered Johnny's peephole. "Maybe we should," Johnny said.

"Okay." Kathy blinked back tears. She realized that she'd been trying to do the mature thing and talk about the problem, but she'd been secretly hoping Johnny would say Cheryl meant nothing to him. "I guess we're breaking up then."

"I guess we are." Johnny's voice was soft. He leaned over and kissed her—on the cheek, which pretty much said it all. "You're a nice person, Kathy O'Dwyer." He opened the car door and got out.

Kathy stayed where she was, crying. She didn't have any Kleenex, and she wiped at her cheeks with her hands. Two months of dating and all she got was "nice." The compliment stung. Obviously, nice wasn't what Johnny wanted if he preferred Cheryl, Kathy thought cattily—then felt bad because she *was* a nice person.

After a few minutes, Kathy squared her shoulders. Time to stop sniffling. If she hadn't been willing to break up, then she shouldn't have mentioned it. If she hadn't pushed the issue, Johnny would probably have kept going out with her for weeks.

Kathy put her hand on the door, then stopped. She dreaded going back inside and facing all those curious looks. *If you don't have enough courage to face a bunch of teenagers, how are you going to face enemy fire?* she asked herself harshly. Besides, it was too cold to stay outside in an unheated car. She was reaching for the latch again when the driver-side door opened, and Evan got in.

He had the car keys and started the car right away. The starter whined twice before turning over, despite having had the block heater plugged in the whole time. "Johnny said you wanted to go home."

Kathy nodded, not trusting her voice. She hoped he couldn't see her wet cheeks in the dimness. Of course, Evan was probably used to girls crying over his brother.

Kathy hated being one of those girls who cried.

Evan got out of the car again to scrape the frost off the windows. It took him several tries just to chip a hole. The thickness of the frost made Kathy vaguely uneasy. The windows had been clear when she and Johnny first came out. How long had she been sitting in the car?

The air blasting out of the defrost vents was finally warm enough to melt the ice that had formed on the inside of the windows by the time Evan climbed back in the car. "That should do it." He backed out of the driveway.

Kathy cleared her throat. If Evan didn't know yet, he would by tomorrow. "Did Johnny tell you we broke up?"

"Yeah."

Another silence fell, as awkward as the first.

"Are you okay?" Evan asked finally.

"I'll be fine," Kathy said, and she would be. Johnny hadn't been the right one for her, that was all. She hadn't even been crying over Johnny, really. She'd cried because rejection hurt.

The guard at the gate recognized the car and waved them through onto the base.

"There's a new Steven Spielberg movie playing Saturday," Evan said as he parked on the street in front of her house. "Would you like to go with me?"

Kathy's mouth dropped open. "You mean, on a date?"

Evan gripped the steering wheel. "Yes, on a date. I like you, Kathy. I have for quite awhile."

"You like me? Does Johnny know about this?" Kathy's thoughts were spinning.

"Oh, Johnny knows all right." Evan looked grim.

"What do you mean by that?" Was this why Johnny had gone along with the breakup? Had he stepped aside in his brother's favour? But Johnny hadn't denied that he liked Cheryl better than Kathy.

Evan laughed harshly. "To hell with it." He turned and looked Kathy directly in the eye. "Johnny's always known that I like you. Do you know why he asked you out?"

Kathy's chin lifted. "I know about the bet, yes, but Johnny could have proposed to any girl. He—"

Evan cut her off. "He asked you out because he knew I planned to. We were lab partners, remember? He didn't even know your name until I made the mistake of dropping your phone number on the floor. He picked it up and said, 'Kathy O'Dwyer? Is that the new base commander's daughter?'"

Tears slipped down Kathy's cheeks, but Evan didn't stop, too angry to even notice.

"No one answered when I tried to phone you that night, and the next day my brother proposed to you in the hall." Bitterness hardened Evan's face. "That morning he asked me if I trusted him. I said if I couldn't trust my brother then who could I trust? We were standing outside the school doors, under the eaves, and a whole row of icicles crashed down—almost skewered me. Johnny pushed me out of the way, then told me I'd be better off trusting a complete stranger. I thought it was a joke. Stupid me. He asked you out to hurt me. That was his only reason. *To hurt me.*"

Kathy felt sick, her pride suffering a blow. *Johnny had never liked her.*

No. She had only Evan's word for that. He might be lying or wrong. Kathy struggled to think it through. She wasn't the type of girl guys fought over, but she had trouble believing Johnny would deliberately try to hurt his brother. "Why would Johnny want to hurt you?"

Evan sighed and the anger left his expression. "It's this thing Johnny does. Ever since our parents died, he's afraid to let anyone get too close. If someone gets close, it's like he has to prove that he doesn't really care, so he pulls some stunt." Evan looked at her. "I thought he'd done something like that to you. I thought that's why you two broke up."

Kathy's chin went up. "Actually, I broke up with him."

Evan's expression lightened. "Yeah, that's what gave me hope. So... will you go out with me on Saturday?"

Kathy closed her eyes. "This is too much... what you've told me... breaking up. I need to think about this."

"I'll take that as a no," Evan said. His jaw set. "You're still hung up on Johnny."

Kathy looked at him and remembered that she had liked him when they first became lab partners. What would have happened if he had asked her out first? Would she ever have even looked at Johnny?

"It's a no for now," Kathy said, "and a maybe for later. If you really like me, ask me again in two weeks." She touched his hand and slid out of the car.

❄ ❄ ❄ ❄

Johnny knew that Frost was unhappy with him. Frost hadn't made an appearance, but he'd made his disapproval perfectly clear when he'd iced the car.

Frost hadn't wanted Johnny to break up with Kathy.

Johnny broke into a grin. But Kathy had broken up with him, so Frost couldn't blame him.

Frost no longer had access the airbase. A good thing.

It almost made up for the other thing. The thing Johnny was trying very hard not to think about, the purchase Frost had forced Johnny to make earlier that day.

CHAPTER 9

-27 °C (-16 °F)

I WILL NOT LOOK AT MY WATCH, Cheryl vowed. *I will not look at my watch.* The empty plastic cup she was holding began to crack in her hand. It was no business of hers exactly how long Kathy and Johnny had been out necking in his car.

She had a headache, and she wanted to go home.

And then Johnny came back in. Alone.

As Cheryl watched, he went over to Evan and said something that made Evan look surprised. Evan put on his coat and left, but Johnny rejoined the party, smiling like a maniac. "Hey, Minik, I bet you I can identify what everyone's drinking with my eyes closed. Loser skates twenty laps tomorrow."

What was going on?

Cheryl wanted badly to go over and ask, but held herself back. Five minutes later, her patience was rewarded.

"I heard him tell Evan that Kathy broke up with him," Tracy told her over the pretzel bowl. "Can you believe it?"

Cheryl had been expecting them to break up since their first date. She wanted to smile, she wanted to laugh, she wanted to turn cartwheels... "Wait a second." Cheryl's eyes narrowed. "Kathy broke up with him? Not the other way around?"

"That's what he told Evan."

Cheryl frowned. "Did he say why?"

"No, but he doesn't seem too sad about it," Tracy said.

Cheryl followed her gaze over to where Johnny was sitting. There were six cups lined up in front of him, and a fringed red scarf had been tied over his eyes while he performed a "taste test" on the various beverages. He swirled and sniffed a cup of cola as if he were a wine connoisseur. "Ah, champagne of a very young vintage. August 2006, if I'm not mistaken—and I never am. Very sweet grapes that year."

Minik, grinning, poured some of the beer someone always managed to sneak in into one cup and handed it to Johnny. "Try this one. Double or nothing."

Johnny went through the whole tasting routine again, making elaborate faces of disgust. "Dog piss," he declared, then corrected himself. "No, no, my mistake." He took another large swallow. "Caribou piss."

For the rest of the evening, Johnny was the life of the party. Cheryl watched from the edges, gradually getting closer as the hour got later and the party dwindled and shrank.

Johnny got more wound up as the night wore on. He did an impression of Don Cherry that had Tracy and Brendan howling with laughter. Cheryl laughed, too, almost helplessly, but the longer she watched his performance—and it was a performance, an act for somebody, though for whom Cheryl couldn't guess—the more uneasy she became. She felt as if she were watching a candle down to the last inch of wick, burning brightly, but drowning in hot wax and about to go out.

Then at three a.m. Brendan and Tracy reluctantly stood up to go. Their host yawned and looked at his watch, obviously ready to call it a night, and Cheryl surprised a look of desperation on Johnny's face.

He doesn't want to be alone, she realized.

Johnny opened his mouth. In another second Cheryl knew he would suggest they all do something crazy—go snowmobiling in the dark, pack a wall of snow in front of the school doors and freeze it solid, something.

Pity stirred in her heart. She spoke first before he could. "Walk me home, Johnny."

Brendan froze in the middle of putting on his jacket, one arm in and one arm out. He and Tracy exchanged a glance.

Cheryl ignored them. Her eyes held Johnny's. "Please."

"Sure," Johnny said, smiling easily as if her request was perfectly normal and not fraught with meaning.

Tracy looked worried. "Are you sure you know what you're doing?" she whispered to Cheryl as they pulled on their coats.

Johnny had already broken her heart once, and he was on the rebound. Cheryl wasn't sure what she was doing at all, but she nodded anyway. She just knew she couldn't bear to leave Johnny alone tonight. She felt a flash of irrational anger at Kathy for having broken up with him and putting Cheryl in this spot.

"Okay," Tracy whispered. Then, in a more normal tone, she and Brendan said goodnight.

And Cheryl was alone with Johnny.

"Hmm," Johnny said as they stepped down off the porch. "I seem to have wheels after all. Evan must have dropped the car off again and then gotten a ride home with someone else. Can I offer you a ride in my chariot?" He made a sweeping bow, indicating the beat-up old blue car.

Even in the cold weather, Cheryl would have preferred to walk, but supposed they couldn't just leave the car there. Despite Johnny's crazy mood, she knew he was perfectly sober—he'd once told her he would never let alcohol mess up his chances for an NHL career. Silently, she got in the passenger side.

The engine started on the first try. Johnny tapped his bare fingers on the steering wheel as he pulled onto the road. He opened his mouth several times, but then didn't seem to know how to say what he wanted.

Cheryl took pity on him again. "It's okay, Johnny. We can park somewhere and talk. I won't assume that it means we're getting back together or anything."

"Reading my mind again?" Johnny looked troubled. "Are you sure? You wouldn't mind?"

Cheryl shrugged. "I'm awake. If you go home like this, you'll just end up waking your brother up and talking his ear off. Consider it a favour to Evan."

Johnny accepted that. He talked about the party as they drove to the skating rink and parked in the icy lot. Then he talked about hockey, giving her a play-by-play of the NHL game that had been on last night. His voice was filled with passion as he expounded on why the Toronto Maple Leafs were his favourite team and the strengths and weaknesses of various goalies.

Listening, Cheryl was both amused and filled with tenderness. The other kids knew Party-Johnny and Future-NHL-Superstar-Johnny, but only she—and maybe Evan—knew Afraid-to-Be-Alone-Johnny. Her feelings were dangerous because they made her feel close to Johnny, but he hadn't changed. She still couldn't trust him.

Johnny's fingers continued to drum on the steering wheel or make staccato gestures. He was so *alive* Cheryl's blood pumped faster just looking at him. He was also scared of something, and she would have given anything for him to be able to tell her what.

Not once in the two hours they sat there did Johnny mention Kathy. Cheryl couldn't decide if that was significant or not. She hoped not.

Finally, around five a.m., Johnny started to run down. "I better get you home," he said, "or your grandfather's going to make boots out of my hide."

Cheryl's grandfather liked Johnny; the idea of him being angry at anybody made Cheryl smile. She yawned. "Okay."

Johnny glanced sideways at her as he put the car into drive. "Thanks, Cheryl. I'd forgotten how good at listening you are. This was... nice."

Cheryl smiled, fully expecting that to be the end of it. Johnny would drop her back at home. By Monday he'd be dating someone else and that would be it.

"Maybe we could do this again sometime." Johnny sounded uncharacteristically tentative.

Cheryl blinked in surprise.

"I mean, we can't date or anything." Johnny gave her a bittersweet smile. "You were right about that. There are way too many polar bears out there, and I can't risk you getting eaten."

"You mean, you'll be leaving soon to play hockey down south and it hurts too much to lose someone you care about," Cheryl interpreted, voice flat.

"Yes," Johnny said after a pause. "So no dating. But maybe we could spend a day together, just having fun. What do you think? You have any plans for tomorrow?"

Cheryl listened in growing disbelief and then anger. "Gee, Johnny, what a generous offer. But I think I'm going to have to say, *No!*"

Her sudden anger didn't faze Johnny. "Ah, come on. Say yes. Just one day," he coaxed. "One day ought to be safe if we keep it light."

"I'm not your convenience. You can't just look me up every time you're between girlfriends," Cheryl said heatedly. This had been a big mistake.

"So you're saying no?"

"Yes!"

Johnny grinned. "Changed your mind already?"

"I mean, yes I'm saying no," Cheryl explained through gritted teeth. She'd forgotten how crazy Johnny could drive her.

"I don't know." Johnny shook his head mockingly. "You sound confused. Let me see if I can persuade you." He stepped on the gas so they shot across the empty parking lot, then suddenly jerked the wheel so they skidded and spun around in a perfect doughnut.

Cheryl let out a small scream and clutched the dash.

"What do you say?" Johnny asked. "Just one day. No kissing, I promise." He crossed his heart as if that were some kind of enticement.

"No—" Cheryl didn't get any further. He spun another doughnut, sending them careening through the dark. "Ack—" She closed her eyes, but that made it worse.

"Changed your mind yet?"

Prudently, Cheryl didn't answer.

"Ah, a tough nut to crack." Johnny sounded delighted at the prospect of a challenge.

He spun five more doughnuts in a row until Cheryl was laughing and dizzy. "Okay, okay, you win," she gasped. "We can spend tomorrow together as friends, but make it stop spinning!"

"No problem." With perfect control, Johnny took the car out of the skid and drove sedately out of the parking lot. "You won't regret this," he told her when they arrived at her house.

I already do, Cheryl thought, but she didn't back out, because she wanted to spend time with Johnny even if it was only for a day. The miserable truth was she loved him. She had survived the Year of the Three Funerals, but she hadn't started to enjoy life again until she'd started dating Johnny.

You liked the way sniffing gasoline made you feel, too, a voice in the back of her head said. Raven's voice. *Johnny is like gasoline; he makes you feel good, but he is no good for you. You know you can't trust him.*

Shut up, she told Raven. *I don't care. I want my day.*

❄ ❄ ❄ ❄

Johnny's sense of peace lasted until he got home and saw the shopping bag by his bed. Compulsively, he went over to it and looked inside at the purchase Frost had made him make that afternoon; the purchase that had made him so nervous and full of energy tonight.

It was a clock. A plain, no frills digital clock. Green numbers proclaimed it to be 5:23 a.m. since Frost had made him purchase batteries, too.

Why did Frost want a clock? Johnny tried to think it through. Say you're Lord of the North, Master of Snow and Ice. You are powerful. You can change the temperature at will, inhabit the heart of a polar bear, send scouring wind and snow. But none of that was enough because what you really need is a clock.

The thing was that Frost couldn't get the clock himself. He seemed to be only intermittently solid and not many people could see him. In order to get a clock, Frost needed a minion. Johnny.

Johnny had always known that Frost had forced him to stay in Iqaluit for a reason, that there was something Frost needed from him. He just hadn't expected it to be a clock.

Johnny looked at the clock again. It showed 5:26 a.m.

See? It's just a clock. Nothing to lose sleep over, Johnny told himself.

But as he lay in bed and closed his eyes he kept seeing the clock's green numbers. Only in his mind, the numbers were counting down toward some nameless doom.

CHAPTER 10

-19 °C (-3 °F)

CHERYL HAD FULLY EXPECTED Johnny to cancel or show up with five other people in tow for safety, but he was on her doorstep at eleven the next morning. Alone.

Cheryl's grandfather didn't ask any questions when Johnny showed up. He accepted Johnny's presence as if it had only been yesterday instead of two months since they'd last seen one another.

His acceptance was one of the things that Cheryl loved about her grandfather. If Aunt Wanda had been home, she would have scowled at Johnny and given him a hard time.

In addition to exercising the regular dog sled team, Grandfather was training some six-month-old pups. She and Johnny joined him out on the tundra and spent two hours working under his mild directions. One white-and-gray pup did not want to learn the commands for turning right and left. All he wanted to do was romp and wrestle with Johnny, pulling off his gloves and playing tug-of-war.

Johnny laughed, but Grandfather shook his head. "That dog is no good. See the others? They like to pull. That dog only wants to play. He was sick as a pup, now he thinks he's a pet, not a working dog."

"He might not be a worker, but he's a good fellow," Johnny said, rubbing the pup's head.

"You like him? I give him to you. He will make a good pet," Grandfather said.

Cheryl looked up sharply. The pup was a handful, but she had seen her grandfather train other dogs with much worse behavioural problems.

"Oh, no, I couldn't," Johnny said at once, but to Cheryl's ears he sounded wistful.

"He is no good to me. You take him."

Johnny continued to say no, but Grandfather wouldn't hear of it. He also turned conveniently deaf when Johnny mentioned payment. "You'd be doing me a favour, taking a no good dog off my hands."

Aunt Wanda would be angry that Grandfather was giving away such an expensive dog, a purebred Siberian husky, but Cheryl held her peace. They were Grandfather's dogs to give, and the expression on Johnny's face... He looked moved almost to tears.

Maybe a dog would help keep Johnny from feeling so alone.

While she watched, Johnny looked deep into the pup's eyes. After a moment, he and the dog seemed to come to an understanding. "You love the cold, don't you?" Johnny murmured, his hands deep in the husky's double-layered fur. "A true creature of the north. He can't possibly object to you."

If Cheryl were Johnny, it was his Aunt Pat's reaction she'd be worrying about, not his Uncle Dan's, but she didn't say so. "So what are you going to name him?" she asked. Guys usually went for macho names. "White Lightning? Winter? Ice?"

Johnny looked at her reproachfully. "Don't be silly. He's obviously a Snowball."

For a moment Cheryl was fooled. "He isn't going to be a puppy forever, you know. He's probably going to get as big as his father, Shadow." She pointed to the big team's lead dog, waiting patiently for his next instruction.

"You're right. What do you think of Earnest?" Johnny asked as the pup gamboled about them.

"More like Happy Go Lucky," Cheryl said, studying the pup.

"Herman? No, wait, I know, Chester. Or maybe Vern."

"You're not naming him Chester," Cheryl said at once. They argued over the pup's name on the walk back to town, eventually settling on Samwise.

They had lunch at Cheryl's. Johnny gamely sat on the kitchen floor with them and ate the pieces of raw fish Grandfather hacked off with a knife, though he didn't put away nearly as much as Cheryl had seen him do with hamburgers and fries. She grinned at him.

Afterward, it seemed natural for Cheryl to walk with Johnny and the pup to his house. He left Cheryl in his front yard with the frisky pup while he went inside. "Aunt Pat, come outside. I have something to show you," she heard him call.

When he came out again, he had Pat Vander Zee in tow. Her eyes were closed, and she was letting Johnny lead her, expression both tolerant and rueful.

He put her hand in the dog's fur, and Samwise licked her face. "I'm guessing it's a dog." She opened her eyes.

"This is Samwise. Samwise say hello to Aunt Pat. She knows where there are good things to eat. If I were you, I'd kiss up to her."

Samwise cocked his head and panted.

Pat looked up sharply. "This is your dog?"

"Unless you or Uncle Dan object," Johnny said steadily.

Pat held his gaze a moment. "You really want him? Dogs take a lot of attention."

"I really want him." Johnny grinned. "Evan will be happy that I have a new running partner."

"Then you have my permission. You'll still have to ask your uncle." She looked back at the dog. "Well, he's certainly a handsome fellow. He can come in the porch, but not in the house." She immediately got up and got out some steel bowls to use as temporary food and water dishes and asked Cheryl's advice on the pup's diet.

Johnny looked at his watch. "It's almost time for hockey practice. We should go."

Johnny, Cheryl knew, never missed hockey practice. Evan wasn't as dedicated. "I have homework," he said shortly when Johnny knocked on his door.

Halfway to the car, Johnny snapped his fingers. "I almost forgot." He ran into the house and came out with a strange-looking pair of skates.

"What are those for?" Cheryl asked.

Johnny looked mischievous. "You'll find out. You are coming to the practice, aren't you?" he asked Cheryl. Wheedled. "I don't want the day to end yet."

You're being foolish, Cheryl's head told her, but she said yes anyhow. They stopped off briefly at her house to grab her skates and then drove to the skating rink.

"Wait." Johnny grabbed her hand when she would have gotten out of the car in the parking lot. "Listen."

On the radio, Cheryl recognized the opening chords of their song, Winter of My Heart. *"Before I met you, I was always cold..."*

They listened in silence for two verses. When the female vocalist hit the chorus, Johnny leaned closer. Cheryl wanted to run her fingers through his hair. "I know we agreed no kissing, but do you think we could make one exception?" He sounded wistful.

Cheryl hardened her heart, reached for the door handle. "I don't think that's a very good idea."

"I'm so cold," Johnny said, green eyes intense. "I need you to warm me, just for a little while."

Cheryl's heartbeat sped up; she tried to kill the feeling with amusement. "Only you would compare me to a fire."

Johnny cocked his head to one side. "Why do you say that?"

"After three funerals, I'm more like ashes or burnt embers," Cheryl said bluntly. Johnny wasn't the only one who was afraid to care too much.

Johnny shrugged. "You can still burn your fingers if you try to pick up a coal, and if you blow on it a bit—" he blew in her ear, lighting up her nerve endings, "—sometimes you get a flame. Come on, Meekitjuk, burn me up. I dare you."

Cheryl wasn't sure just who lit the match, but they definitely caught fire, kissing until some other members of the hockey team showed up and honked.

Johnny laughed and waved good-naturedly, his arm still around Cheryl. Cheryl glimpsed Brendan and Tracy, but most of her attention was still focused on Johnny. It felt good to be in his arms again. So good that Cheryl felt alarmed. She'd given up on Johnny. This sudden turnabout couldn't be real.

"We'd better go in," Johnny said. "It's safer in a crowd."

Cheryl was the only spectator.

"I can't stay," Tracy told her, "I have to go to the library to work on a report, but I'll come back afterward." She paused. "Well?"

Cheryl smiled blandly.

"Are you and Johnny going out again?" Tracy asked.

"I don't know. Maybe."

Tracy looked skeptical, but left.

"Hey, Johnny, let's see you do those forty laps you owe me for losing the bet last night," Minik called.

"How about a side bet?" Johnny pulled the strange-looking pair of skates out of his hockey bag. "If I do all forty skating on my uncle's Dutch skates, then you have to do twenty laps."

The antique Dutch skates looked more like a piece of wood with a blade strapped to the bottom than regular skates. The blade was about six inches longer than normal and the wood curled up at the end. They had no boot, only some straps. "You'll trip over your feet on those things," Minik said. "You're on!"

Johnny, of course, did no such thing. He made skating with the Dutch blades look so easy that Minik insisted on trying them when his turn came. Minik fell five times in one circuit and demanded his own skates back.

Even once their hockey coach arrived and set the team to doing a bunch of drills, Johnny kept clowning around. He had such a good time that only someone very observant would have noticed that he also worked harder than everyone else, skating with amazing speed. Cheryl felt a pang watching. He really did belong in a bigger league. Iqaluit wouldn't be able to hold him for much longer.

She noticed Dan Vander Zee slip in and watch for a few minutes and figured he probably knew it, too.

After practice, Cheryl found out why Johnny had gotten her to take her skates. About half the team and Tracy and Cheryl hung around for a game of Crack-the-whip. Since Cheryl didn't have a helmet, Johnny insisted on giving her his and going bareheaded himself.

Minik and a husky defenceman formed the anchor in the centre of the ice for the game to pivot around. Everyone joined hands, making a line of nine. Johnny linked first, then Cheryl. She ended up third from the whip end.

Everyone skated in a large circle around the pivot. After two complete rotations, the line had picked up enough momentum that Cheryl didn't have to skate. She was pulled along by the other skaters in a dizzying circle. The farther down the chain you were, the faster you went and the farther you travelled.

A small scream escaped Cheryl as they swung round the first corner, largely drowned out by Brendan's whoop and Tracy's louder shriek. Johnny pulled on Cheryl's left hand, and Tracy pulled on her right. Cheryl struggled to hold on, but Tracy began to slip free. For a heart-stopping moment, Cheryl thought she would go with Tracy, but Johnny's grip on her hand stayed strong, almost bruisingly so. "I've got you."

Tracy and Brendan sailed free. Brendan braked easily, but, like Cheryl, Tracy had never mastered the T-stop and had to put out her arms to avoid smashing into the boards. Then they quickly skated to center ice and joined the pivot end of the chain to become pullers.

Cheryl found herself at the end of the line; both the most dangerous and most thrilling position on the chain. At its end Cheryl got the benefit of the widest swing, but if anyone's grip broke she would go flying.

"Switch grips," Johnny shouted as they headed into the next corner.

Obediently, Cheryl locked her fingers around Johnny's wrist, and Johnny did the same to her wrist, resulting in a stronger double-grip. She needed it. At the end of the line, the speed was faster, increasing the strain on her arm.

She was smiling, laughing even, when somebody halfway up the stands caught her eye. Sharp white face, pointy chin, silver hair like dripping icicles and pit-dark eyes.

The line pulled her away before she could be sure, but Cheryl was instinctively certain it was The Stranger. She looked back, but couldn't spot him again.

Couldn't, that is, until she faced forward and saw him standing a quarter of the way around the rink from where he'd been moments ago, only this time he was closer to ice level.

He was looking at her. There was nothing of mercy in his eyes. No human warmth, not even anger.

A shock of cold went through Cheryl. "Johnny," she started to say, but Johnny was swearing. Cheryl's eyes snapped wide-open as the side of the rink loomed in front of them.

The pullers had misjudged. Instead of skimming the side of the boards Cheryl was going to crash into them.

They were going so fast... She wanted to close her eyes, but kept watching in horror, certain that in a second she would squish against the boards like rotten fruit.

Then Johnny's grip on her wrist tightened, and he pulled her in closer instead, with inhuman strength. One of her shoulders touched his, and the other grazed the boards.

They were past.

Cheryl had just taken a breath of relief when The Stranger appeared on the ice, right in front of her.

She cried out and tried to let go of Johnny, but his fingers bit into her wrist, and it was too late, she ran into The Stranger. Instead of colliding with him, she went through him—needles of ice pricked her skin, like standing naked in a snowstorm—and screamed again, whipping along so fast, out of control—

Her mitten came off in Johnny's hand.

Cheryl spun off the chain toward the boards. Whizzing. Much too fast for Cheryl's simple snowplow to have any effect. She smashed head-first into the boards. Her too-large helmet tumbled off.

The last thing she heard was The Stranger's cold laughter.

❄ ❄ ❄ ❄

When Cheryl opened her eyes again, her head hurt fiercely. She felt muzzy and disoriented. Time seem to jump forward in fits and starts:

—lying on the ice, cold and uncomfortable, Johnny's face looming over hers, and then it wasn't Johnny's face at all, but The Stranger's, white and cruel, bloodless as a corpse's, and she recoiled, screaming, and cracked her head on the ice a second time—

—bumping and jolting in a car, a moving car, her head on someone's lap, not Johnny's, Tracy's, feeling sick and turning her head and vomiting on the floor—

—light shining in her eyes, a doctor asking her questions and announcing that she had a concussion—

—Tracy, angry, "I can't believe Johnny didn't come with you to the hospital. I hope you dump him, like Kathy did."

—then Aunt Wanda was there, holding her hand and saying everything was going to be just fine—

—and then it was dark and Cheryl cried out in pain and fright, not knowing where she was for a moment, and someone stepped forward into the half-light from the hall. She cringed back until she saw it was Johnny. Or maybe it wasn't. His face was in shadow, and her head hurt so. Maybe Johnny was just her imagination...

❄ ❄ ❄ ❄

Johnny thought Cheryl had been awake and aware of him for a moment, but she was unconscious now. He'd deliberately waited until the nurses had given her more pain meds before slipping into her room.

He couldn't face her if she was conscious. He could barely face her like this, lying on a narrow hospital bed. She looked so haggard and ill.

"I'm so sorry," he told her. His ragged breathing made the words come out hoarse and too loud. "It's my fault you were hurt. I thought it would be okay to spend today together as long as we didn't talk about anything deep." Johnny's hands clenched into fists. "But apparently that wasn't the point."

"Apparently the point Frost wants to make is that I can't have you." He laughed briefly, without humour. "Big surprise. I'm not even allowed a pal like Kathy. Uncle Dan gave up on me years ago. Aunt Pat never wanted us in the first place. Evan's mad at me again. Who's left? I hate being alone."

CHAPTER 11

-30 °C (-22 °F)

"CAN I TALK TO YOU AFTER CLASS TODAY?" Evan asked.

"Sure," Kathy said without thinking. Then she registered how nervous Evan looked and realized that exactly two weeks had passed since she and Johnny broke up.

Did he intend to ask her out? Kathy's pulse fluttered. Although she and Evan had continued to be Chemistry lab partners, they'd been very careful to only talk about school or the weather. Evan hadn't flirted at all, and Kathy had almost decided that he'd changed his mind about liking her.

It had been a very strange two weeks. Kathy had mostly kept her head down, ignoring the gossip that swirled around her and Johnny and Cheryl.

The gossip had been especially fierce the day Cheryl returned to school, having recovered from her concussion. Cheryl had worn her usual stone face, but Kathy had been watching Johnny. When he first saw Cheryl again, he'd frozen for an instant, staring at her.

Kathy had had the disturbing idea that Johnny was only pretending to be fine, that he was actually acutely miserable. Then he'd looked away and helped himself to Brendan's banana. In the laughing squabble that followed the brief impression had shattered.

Cheryl had taken a seat far away from both Johnny and Kathy. They could have been the three points of an equilateral triangle.

"First I'd like to apologize," Evan said once the lab had cleared of people. "I shouldn't have told you the only reason Johnny was dating you was because of me. He may not have realized who you were until after he'd asked you out. Or he might have liked you without knowing your name." Evan smiled crookedly. "I never could tell what Johnny was thinking."

"Me either," Kathy said ruefully.

Evan took a deep breath. His brown eyes were direct. "Anyhow, I'd like to try again. Would you like to go to the movies tonight? With me, I mean?"

His nervousness bemused her. She couldn't remember a guy being nervous that she'd say no before. Johnny had always had a high gloss of confidence, his ego impossible to dent. Evan cared what her answer was. "All right," Kathy said softly. If it was a mistake, she'd know soon enough.

Evan picked her up exactly on time—very different than Johnny who ran chronically late unless it involved hockey.

"So what movie do you want to see?" Kathy asked once they were in the car. Iqaluit had four movie screens.

"What movie do you want to see?" Evan countered. "There's a new romantic comedy playing."

On the verge of saying that was fine by her, Kathy stopped. "Actually, I tend to like action movies better than chick flicks."

"You do?" Evan looked surprised and pleased.

They ended up seeing the latest Jackie Chan movie and were having an animated discussion over which stunt had been the best, when Johnny came up behind them and clapped Evan on the shoulder. "Hey, bro. How's it going?"

Kathy tensed, worried that her dating Evan might drive a wedge between the two brothers, but Johnny quickly made it clear he bore no grudge, and she relaxed.

"You two look good together," Johnny said after a minute's light conversation. "Just make sure you return Kathy before curfew or her dad will come after you with a squadron," he teased Evan.

Evan looked a little dazed when Johnny left. "Well, that went better than I expected. Do I really have to worry about your dad?"

Kathy laughed. "Not if you get me home on time. My dad will want to meet you though. Mom, too."

There was one awkward moment when Kathy made the introductions. "Mom, Dad, this is Evan Vander Zee."

Her parents exchanged startled looks. Belatedly, Kathy realized that, though she'd told them she was going out with Evan and had probably mentioned his name before, her parents hadn't known Evan was Johnny's brother until now. Her mom, she sensed, was planning a heart to heart with her later, but her dad just went on to the next question in his inquisition. "So, Evan, what do you intend to do after you graduate?"

Evan's answer surprised Kathy a little. "I'm going to go to university and take civil engineering."

For some reason she had assumed that Evan was as serious about hockey as Johnny was. She asked him about it when they went into the den to watch music videos. "No NHL dreams for you?"

"No. Even if I wanted to, I'm not good enough," Evan said simply.

"But you drill with Johnny all the time," Kathy protested. Too late, she wished she hadn't mentioned Johnny.

But Evan just groaned. "Don't remind me. He had me up at 6 a.m. this morning, shooting pucks. I was barely awake; it was dark and colder than hell. We were out there for an hour, drilling, and he was still going strong when I went inside. If it wasn't for Johnny, I wouldn't play hockey at all." He grimaced.

Kathy was curious. "Why do you play hockey if you don't like it?"

Evan hesitated. "To be close to Johnny. When we were kids he liked hockey, but, after our parents died, he practically lived on the small rink Uncle Dan flooded for him. If I was playing hockey with him, at least we were doing something together." Evan paused.

"Besides, hockey is Johnny's dream. If practicing with him helps him make it to the NHL, then it's worth a few early mornings. He's really good, you know," Evan said softly.

Kathy knew. There was a kind of glory to Johnny when he was on the ice. It was as if he became part of it. "If a scout sees him, he'll get snapped up."

"That's what I think, too." Evan hesitated. "But sometimes I worry about what will happen if he doesn't get drafted, or he gets injured. Johnny doesn't have a backup plan."

"No, he wouldn't," Kathy agreed. "Not his style."

"Anyway, enough about my brother."

They talked about school for an hour. Kathy kept waiting for Evan to kiss her, but he didn't, and then it was time for him to go home.

Kathy's pulse picked up as she walked him to the door. Surely now he'd kiss her.

Evan put on his boots and gloves and zipped up his coat. "I'll go start the car, then come back in for a minute while it warms up."

A blast of frigid air hit the porch as he went out and another one arrived when he came back in. Kathy shivered, but came down two steps so she wouldn't tower over him.

Evan pushed back his hood and took off his gloves. "Man, it's cold. I don't know about you, but I'm getting tired of thirty below weather and it's only November."

Kathy agreed that she wished it would warm up at least enough to go snowmobiling. She'd just decided, disappointed, that Evan wasn't going to kiss her at all, and had said goodbye and was turning away, when he made his move. They bumped noses and missed lips.

Evan gave a small laugh. "Sorry. I guess I'm a little nervous."

"Because I used to date Johnny?" Kathy asked carefully, when Evan didn't try again. Her stomach hollowed out. She'd had a good time tonight, but if Evan was eaten up with jealousy then maybe this had been a mistake after all.

"Sort of. Johnny's very popular with... I mean, he's had lots of girlfriends and I haven't." Evan looked miserable.

He didn't sound jealous so much as insecure. Kathy took a chance and told him the truth. "I don't think Johnny was that attracted to me. He usually kissed me on the forehead. I was starting to wonder if I had bad breath."

Evan got his courage up then. "I'd rather kiss you on the lips." Kathy was still one step higher than him, so he cupped his hand around the back of her neck and pulled her down for a kiss. "You taste pretty good to me," he said after a long breathless moment. He smiled, looking both shy and pleased with himself. "No bad breath."

In the living room, her dad cleared his throat, and Evan quickly said goodbye and left.

Over the next month, Kathy found dating Evan to be a much quieter prospect than dating Johnny had been. And that was fine. They did things together—movies, snowmobiling, board games, tobogganing, lunch dates—without always travelling in a large group.

Practically the only time she saw Johnny was in English class and at hockey games when he would smile or say hi in passing.

She never noticed anything wrong.

❀ ❀ ❀ ❀

"Johnny." Uncle Dan waited until Johnny stopped drumming his fingers and looked up at him. "I've made a decision."

Johnny waited incuriously.

"You can start junior hockey after Christmas. I've talked to your coach and he's making some calls. We'll know which team in a few days."

Johnny should have been elated. Junior hockey, the first stepping stone to the NHL, his dream—instead he felt nothing. "That's great," he said, but even to his own ears he sounded unenthusiastic. Uncle Dan and Aunt Pat, who was hovering in the doorway, dishcloth in hand, looked disappointed. He tried again. "I'm looking forward to it."

But he wasn't. He no longer believed Frost would let him leave.

Uncle Dan wanted to talk about it some more, what teams he was most likely to play for and how he would be expected to keep up his grades—and Johnny couldn't stand it. He got to his feet. "If I'm going to play junior hockey, I guess I better go practice some more." Even though it was 10 p.m. he grabbed his equipment and escaped outside.

It felt like escape. Like leaving prison to be outside under the stars. Lately the only time he felt whole was when he was skating. The rest of the time he just went through the motions.

He'd barely gotten warmed up on the ice when Samwise lifted his head. Johnny looked up and saw Aunt Pat, bundled up from head to toes in a green jacket and ski pants with only a few inches around her eyes and nose showing.

He expected her to urge him to come inside out of the bitter -30 °C weather, but she surprised him. "Johnny, what's wrong?"

"Nothing." He shot a puck into the empty net, with a nice easy wrist shot. Always a wrist shot. Never the more flashy slap shot. Control was the name of the game.

"Dan and I thought you'd be excited about moving south and starting junior hockey. One of the reasons we decided to let you go after all is because we're worried about you... your attitude lately. We were hoping this would snap you out of your depression."

"I'm not depressed." Johnny made the mistake of actually looking at his aunt. She stared back at him fearlessly.

"Oh, I think you are, Johnny." She sounded sure. And angry. "You haven't been acting like yourself at all. You never want to go out anymore. All you do is play hockey."

"Maybe I'm growing up," Johnny said flippantly. Anger stirred inside him. "I don't know why you want the old Johnny back. You never liked him much."

"That's not true," Aunt Pat said, but she said it a beat too late.

"First you complain that I party too much, now you're complaining that I don't go out enough. Make up your mind." Johnny shot another puck into the net. Score.

"It's your state of mind we're worried about."

Johnny wanted to question that *we*. Uncle Dan wasn't standing out here in the cold.

"Please tell me what's wrong," Aunt Pat said.

Johnny lost his temper. "You really want to know what's wrong? I'll tell you what's wrong: he's never going to let me go."

Aunt Pat thought he meant Uncle Dan, not Frost. Dismay filled her round face. "Is that what you think? You're wrong. We're not playing mind games with you, Johnny. You really do have our permission to play junior hockey."

"Unless I screw up, you mean," Johnny said. He shouldn't be angry at her, but he was. "And we both know I will. In fact, I can guarantee that I will."

Aunt Pat looked devastated. "Is that how you feel? That we're judging you all the time? Oh, Johnny."

She was struggling against tears, and Johnny felt a gut-punch of remorse. Frost was his problem, not Aunt Pat. "No, I shouldn't have said that. Uncle Dan had every right to punish me. I flipped the snowmobile on purpose," he confessed.

"What? Why?"

Frost suddenly appeared behind Aunt Pat's shoulder. *Be careful what you say, Johnny.*

Samwise raised his hackles and growled.

Suddenly Johnny had had enough. "Why should I be careful?" he shouted at Frost. "Do you really think she'd believe me? Hey, Aunt

Pat, here's the real reason I flipped the snowmobile: because if I didn't do it Evan or Kathy would have been killed."

Aunt Pat was staring at him.

"See?" Johnny told Frost. "She thinks I'm crazy. No harm done. *Now leave me alone.*" He turned back to the ice, but had trouble spotting the puck. His hands were shaking.

He assumed Aunt Pat had gone back to the house, so when she walked out onto the homemade rink and stood in front of him, he felt jolted.

"Johnny, who are you talking to?" She paused. "Is someone threatening you?"

"As a matter of fact someone is. Want to see him?" Johnny asked sarcastically. "He's standing right there." He turned his aunt and pointed in the right direction. Even though Aunt Pat had never seen Frost before, Johnny found himself holding his breath. Cheryl had seen Frost, so had Kathy. Maybe...

Stop this now, Frost commanded.

"There's nothing there," Aunt Pat said firmly, but she shivered.

Johnny's grip tightened on her padded shoulders. He'd known she wouldn't be able to see Frost so why was he so disappointed? "Nothing, huh? Then what's Samwise growling at?"

Aunt Pat glanced around, uneasily. "I don't know. Maybe an arctic hare."

Johnny made himself back away. "Then there's your answer. I am crazy. Why don't you go inside?"

She didn't argue, walking—no, *scurrying*—away. All he'd succeeded in doing was scaring his aunt.

No, not all. He'd also pissed off Frost.

"You should not have taken such a risk," Frost said, his voice a cold north wind. "You know I'll have to punish you now."

CHAPTER 12

-36 °C (-32 °F)

BUTTERFLIES TUMBLED IN KATHY'S STOMACH. Knowing that Kathy's mom was away on a trip, Evan had invited Kathy over to his place for supper, and she was nervous. The last time she'd gone to dinner at the Vander Zees she'd been dating Johnny. "So what do your aunt and uncle think of the whole us-dating thing?" she asked Evan when they'd parked out front of the house.

Evan understood what she meant. "Aunt Pat wasn't sure at first, but Uncle Dan told her that if I wasn't allowed to date Johnny's exes the pool of available girls narrowed considerably."

Kathy laughed. "Okay, then."

Evan paused as if struck by a sudden thought. "What about your parents? Is your mom still worried?"

After their first date, Kathy's mom had cornered her in the kitchen and expressed concern that Kathy and Evan had started dating so quickly. She'd warned Kathy that she might be on the rebound and end up hurting Evan. "Not anymore. She said the other day that we seemed better suited than Johnny and I were." Kathy put on her earmuffs and got out of the car. It was cold and clear and black out. No northern lights tonight. Too bad.

Evan was looking at her with a funny expression. "So you don't miss Johnny at all?"

"No."

"Not even the whole popular thing? Being the center of a party?" Kathy gave his arm a little punch. "No!"

"Sorry, it's just that everybody loves Johnny," Evan said cynically. "Girls want to date him, guys want to be his friend, hockey coaches love having him on their team, even his teachers let him get away with murder. Don't get me wrong. I love Johnny, too, but sometimes it's a pain being his brother."

Kathy cocked her head, listening.

"I mean, Iqaluit wasn't *my* first choice of where I wanted to live, but no one's offered to send me to school in Ontario. Not that I mind anymore," he added hastily.

"Good answer," Kathy told him. "Truthfully, the only thing I miss about your brother is having a training partner."

"Hey, anytime you want me to count your pushups, I'm there for you," Evan offered.

"Really?" Kathy stopped outside the door and looked at him in surprise. "I mean, you've been pretty understanding about all the hours my physical training eats up. Which I appreciate. Wouldn't you get bored?"

"You forget I'm used to dealing with the obsessed," Evan told her dryly. "I'd be happy to keep you company. Just don't expect me to get up at six and run up and down the road with you."

"In this weather? Who would be that crazy?" Kathy did all her running on an exercise machine nowadays.

"Johnny, of course."

"Did he try to drag you out of bed this morning?"

"Not lately. He's got his dog now for that." Evan made a face. "Now if he could just teach Samwise to play hockey with him, too..." He pushed open the door.

The first thing Kathy noticed when she went inside was that Evan's normally elegant aunt was wearing green sweat pants in order to accommodate a white cast on one leg. "What happened?" Kathy asked.

"I slipped on the ice," Pat said. She looked embarrassed. "We always park in the same spot in the yard, so there's a depression where the car sits and the ice slopes down. I lost my balance and slid halfway under the car and managed to break my leg. So now I'm on these stupid crutches, which are useless on the ice. The boys have been putting down rock salt for me, otherwise I'd be trapped in the house."

"Better than being trapped outside," Johnny said. Kathy turned, startled; she hadn't heard him entering the room. "You forgot to mention that you bumped your head and blacked out when you fell. If you'd been stuck under that car for much longer in this weather, you'd have frozen." His voice was curiously flat.

"I was barely out for a minute," Pat said dismissively. "I was just coming to when the dog started howling. You were there right away."

"And if it had happened during the day, when no one was home?" Johnny asked.

"One of the neighbours would have heard me. Or if I'd had to, I could have crawled into the house on my elbows," Pat said stubbornly.

Johnny snorted as if he didn't believe her.

Kathy looked at Evan, confused by the almost argument. Why was Johnny angry?

Evan stepped in. "Well, I'm just glad you didn't have to. You were pretty white, Aunt Pat. I think that's the only time I've ever heard you swear," he teased.

Johnny was uncharacteristically silent at supper, withdrawn, even moody. Evan, Kathy and Pat Vander Zee carried the bulk of the conversation. Even Dan Vander Zee talked more than Johnny.

As soon as his plate was cleared, Johnny shoved back from the table.

"Don't you want dessert?" Pat asked. "I made your favourite, chocolate cheesecake."

Johnny didn't look back. "I'm not hungry."

Pat bit her lip for a moment before asking Kathy if she'd like a slice. Kathy felt angry at Johnny. Couldn't he see that he'd hurt his aunt's feelings? She and Evan both praised the dessert to high heaven as compensation.

It was a relief to escape the tense atmosphere and go study in Evan's room.

"What was the significance of Shakespeare on the Renaissance?" Kathy quizzed Evan for their upcoming Social Studies final.

"There's something I want to show you," Evan said abruptly.

"Wrong," Kathy joked. "His plays were published in a vernacular language instead of Latin."

Evan didn't smile. "I'm serious. Will you come with me?"

Kathy stood up. "Of course."

Evan wouldn't tell her what he wanted to show her, but Kathy had already guessed it wasn't a Christmas present when Evan made her put on her outdoor clothes and led her around back of the house.

Away from the streetlights it was oppressively dark. A yard light sent a cone of light onto a small outdoors rink. Johnny was skating up and down the ice, deftly handling a puck. Every time he passed the net he put a puck into the upper right hand corner.

Samwise trotted over to them, sniffed their hands, then went back to standing guard over Johnny.

"What is it?" Kathy asked, shifting from foot to foot in an effort to stay warm. Her ski pants made an annoying whispery sound as the fabric rubbed together.

"Shh. Watch," Evan said.

Kathy watched. Five pucks into the upper right-hand corner, then five into the upper left. As she watched Johnny do the same drill over and over, never missing, she began to feel uneasy. Although she and Evan were standing right there Johnny never acknowledged them by a look or a wave. He actcd as if only the ice and the puck and the net existed. Kathy had attended many of Johnny's hockey games, and he'd always been focused, but never like this.

"You see it, too," Evan said. "Don't you? Something's wrong with Johnny."

Kathy nodded. She felt frightened. There was something almost inhuman in the way Johnny kept skating so smoothly without evidence of coldness or fatigue or error.

Evan took her back inside, but didn't say anything until they were back in his room. "I'm worried about him. He spends all his spare time out practicing on the ice. He even practices right after we've had a game! I haven't seen him this bad since our parents died. Brendan asked me if there was something wrong yesterday. He says Johnny hasn't been to a party in over a month."

Kathy felt her mouth go dry. Johnny, not go to parties? Johnny loved crowds. That wasn't right.

"Uncle Dan told him he could play junior hockey, but it didn't cheer him up. His grades are going down the toilet. He isn't dating anyone, which, trust me, is a first for my big brother. He doesn't joke anymore. I think he's given up sleeping. Every time I wake up in the middle of the night, his light's on.

Evan stared down at his hands. "Something is very wrong."

"Do you have any idea what the problem might be?" Kathy asked.

Evan shrugged. "I've asked him about a dozen times, but he just shuts me down. Aunt Pat thinks it's because of the dark days—some people get depressed because of the lack of sunlight. She wants to send him to a psychiatrist; she and Uncle Dan had a big argument about it."

Kathy could understand that. Although Iqaluit did not actually lie in the Arctic Circle it was darn close, only about 300 km short of it. Today was December 15, just a week short of the solstice, when sunlight would last for a bare four hours before vanishing behind the curve of the earth. Above the Arctic Circle there would be 24-hour darkness, just as there had been 24-hour sunlight in June.

Kathy found all the darkness weird—but also kind of neat. Seeing stars and northern lights in the afternoon wowed her. The dark combined with the temperature, which had stayed close to -30 °C all month, had kept her mostly cooped up indoors and feeling antsy. Her mom, who wasn't much for outdoor stuff, hardly seemed to notice at all.

"Johnny does like to be outdoors," Kathy offered.

"Yeah, but it's more than that." Evan looked frustrated. "You saw him out there."

"You're right," Kathy agreed. "It gave me the creeps to see him practice like that."

Kathy had never been in love with Johnny, but she discovered now that she still cared about him, and she definitely cared that Evan was worried sick. "How long has Johnny been acting strangely?"

Evan shrugged. "A month, month and a half. I didn't really notice at first because we had just started dating and we weren't hanging around with the same group anymore."

"When was the first time you noticed something odd about his behaviour?"

Evan hesitated. "Actually, the day after you and he broke up. That's when he got Samwise. I asked him where he got the dog— purebred huskies are quite expensive, you know—and he practically took my head off. He said it didn't matter where the dog came from, what mattered was that it was bred for the cold."

Kathy frowned, not sure what to make of that. "Huh."

"Did he ever say anything weird to you?" Evan asked. "While you were dating? I guess I'm just wondering if this has been going on for awhile and I never noticed."

"Not unless you count the time he told me he caught Jack Frost."

To her surprise Evan grinned. "Jack Frost, huh? I remember that night. He stayed up to catch Jack Frost and almost caught pneumonia instead." Evan smiled wryly. "That was the night I saved his life."

"Really?" Kathy leaned forward.

"He told me what he'd planned. He always told me when he was going to catch the Tooth Fairy or the Easter bunny or whatever. I didn't like being left alone in the dark, and I couldn't fall asleep. I waited and waited for him to come back.

"When I couldn't stand it any longer, I woke up Mom and Dad, and we started looking for him. We found him standing in the middle of the yard. Barefoot. In his pajamas. With his tongue stuck to the iron swing-post. He couldn't talk or scream. His toes were red with cold. It was freezing out that night."

Kathy winced in sympathy.

"Mom was horrified. She bundled him up in a blanket and rushed him to the hospital. He should have caught pneumonia, but he didn't. He's immune to the cold."

"Well, that hasn't changed." Kathy looked out the dark window. "Good thing, I guess."

They were both silent for a moment, thinking about Johnny still out there in the cold, practicing.

"Last night, I even went so far as to ask Johnny if he was acting weird because he missed you," Evan admitted. "But he just slapped me on the shoulder and said no, you'd never belonged to him."

"I could have told you that," Kathy said firmly. "Johnny is not pining away out of love for me. The reason we broke up was because Johnny was still in love with Cheryl."

"Cheryl was a long time ago," Evan said doubtfully. "I know I said he didn't like to dance with anyone else to their song, but I always thought that was to spare her feelings."

Kathy shook her head. "If you'd seen them read each other's stories in English class, you wouldn't have any doubt. And don't you remember the gossip going around about the two of them? Tracy told me that Johnny went home with Cheryl the night we broke up."

Evan looked skeptical. "I wouldn't put too much stock in what Tracy Beaumont said either. He probably gave her a lift, that's all."

"Tracy said they were together the next day, too. When Cheryl got her concussion. Maybe we should talk to Cheryl. She might have a chance of getting through the Johnny."

❄ ❄ ❄ ❄

The contents of the shopping bag in Johnny's closet were growing. To the alarm clock had been added a number of wires and electronics. Johnny could no longer convince himself that Frost wanted a clock.

Frost wanted a bomb.

Johnny comforted himself with the knowledge that there were no actual explosives. Nothing in his closet could or would go boom. And when the time came and Frost sent him out to buy dynamite, or the ingredients to make nitroglycerin, Johnny would refuse. Not even to save the life of someone he loved was he going to blow up innocent people. No way. It would end as soon as Frost crossed that line.

It would end there.

Of course, it would.

Faintly, in the back of his mind Johnny heard mocking silvery laughter.

CHAPTER 13

-34 °C (-29 °F)

IF CHERYL HAD MADE A LIST of the people most likely to call her, she would have ranked Kathy O'Dwyer dead last—right after the President of France and the Easter Bunny. Kathy had never made any secret of the fact she didn't like Cheryl. Cheryl wasn't that fond of Kathy either. So it jolted Cheryl to hear her voice on the telephone.

"Cheryl, this is Kathy. Evan and I would like to talk to you. It's about Johnny."

Cheryl's heartbeat jumped, but she kept her voice cool. "What about him?"

"He's been acting odd lately. Evan's worried about him."

"I haven't talked to Johnny in over a month." Concern began to creep into her mind. Acting odd, how? "Did he ask you to speak to me?"

"Uh, no." Kathy killed that hope. "We'd really like to talk to you. Can you come over to my house this afternoon?"

"If you want to talk to me, you can come over here. Evan knows where I live." Cheryl hung up without saying goodbye. Kathy always brought out the worst in her.

"We might get some visitors this afternoon," Cheryl told her grandfather in Inuktitut. Her aunt was working, waitressing.

Her grandfather nodded, but said nothing. He continued mending the dog's harness on the kitchen table. His knobby fingers worked slowly, but with a sureness Cheryl found comforting.

To her surprise, Kathy and Evan knocked on the door a bare fifteen minutes later. Cheryl showed them into the living room. The threadbare brown tweed couch, which folded out into her grandfather's bed, and the mismatched tiger lily print chair made Cheryl feel defensive. She was not a good hostess and did not offer refreshments. "Tell me what you think is wrong with Johnny."

Johnny wasn't ill, she learned with just a little too much relief, though he might be depressed. He was avoiding parties and had become even more obsessed with hockey.

"What about the dog?" Cheryl asked.

Evan looked puzzled. "Samwise? He's fine."

"Johnny still spends time with him?"

"He spends more time with the dog than anyone else. If Samwise was a girl, I'd be expecting them to get engaged," Evan said dryly.

The knowledge eased Cheryl's heart slightly. At least Johnny had the dog. He wasn't completely alone.

Cheryl waited impassively while Evan kept cataloguing differences in Johnny's behaviour. "So why tell me?" she asked when he had finished. Somewhere deep inside she wanted to hear the words: Johnny needs you.

She didn't get her wish.

"We think Johnny's depressed because of seasonal affective disorder—the lack of sunlight," Kathy said, "but he won't talk to Evan. We were hoping maybe you could try. He might open up more to someone outside the family."

Cheryl doubted it. "Johnny's not good at talking."

Kathy looked at her as if she were crazy.

Cheryl ignored her and turned to Evan. "Look, this sunlight thing, I don't know about that. If that's what's bothering him, wouldn't he stay inside?"

Evan shrugged.

"You said this started around the time when he broke up with Kathy?" Cheryl thought back. He hadn't wanted to be alone that night, but he'd seemed his usual Johnny-self the next day, clowning around with the Dutch skates. She couldn't remember exactly how her accident had happened, except that Tracy had said they'd been playing Crack-the-Whip.

A dark memory stirred in the back of her mind like a corpse clawing its way out of a grave.

She followed a hunch. "Do you think Johnny's change of personality might have something to do with The Stranger instead?"

"Who?" Evan asked.

Cheryl turned to Kathy. "The man you saw just before your snowmobile accident. I call him The Stranger."

Kathy's eyes widened. "You saw him, too?"

"Yes, then and one other time." The day she and Johnny had met the polar bear. Both had been mere glimpses, but they'd been more than enough to burn The Stranger into her brain. Both times, she suddenly realized, had been during a time of danger.

"If you saw him, why didn't you say so?" Kathy looked mad.

"I didn't feel like it."

Evan cleared his throat. "I haven't seen any strangers hanging around Johnny—"

Kathy shivered. "If you'd seen this guy, you'd remember him, believe me. Those eyes...."

Something flickered across Evan's face that made Cheryl think he was lying. She'd bet that he had seen The Stranger, too—he just didn't want to remember.

"I don't think I've seen anybody—at least not recently." Evan looked troubled for a moment then shook his head. "But I haven't been looking either. Do you think we should try to find this stranger and talk to him about Johnny?" Evan asked.

No! Cheryl wanted to cry—she was certain down to her soul that trying to talk to The Stranger was a bad idea—but stopped herself from saying the words aloud. Her original conviction that The Stranger was bad magic came crashing back. Her grandfather would understand, but she couldn't find the words to explain it to Kathy and Evan. They were too mired in the modern world to comprehend the old world.

"No," Kathy said, "I think we should stick to our original plan." She looked at Cheryl expectantly. "There's a hockey game this Saturday. You can talk to him then." She got up to go as if Cheryl had already agreed.

Cheryl saw her and Evan out in silence. She would be the one to decide if she went to the game, not Kathy.

Troubled, Cheryl went back into the kitchen. "So what do you think?" she asked her grandfather. She was sure he'd listened to every word.

Her grandfather feigned ignorance. "What do I think about what?"

"About Johnny. Should I give him another chance?" Cheryl slumped down at the table. The last month had been calm. Not happy, but calm.

You mean you've been numb, a voice in the back of her mind said.

Her grandfather lay down the harness. "I think this boy needs you."

"If he needs me, then why did he do all this?" Cheryl demanded. "Break up with me. Date Kathy, but keep phoning me. On Dad's anniversary he took me out onto the ice and held me while I talked about it, but he didn't tell me anything about himself. He didn't let me in."

"Maybe he has been telling you what's wrong and you haven't been listening," her grandfather said.

Cheryl shook her head, but two days later when the hockey game started she was there. She couldn't shake the terrible, illogical feeling that whatever was wrong with Johnny she was the only one who could help him.

It was Dec. 19, the first day of Christmas holidays, so the fans were out in force. Cheryl finally located Kathy squeezed up against the glass in one of the corners. There were still some seats high up, but Kathy had probably decided there was no point in being at the game if Johnny didn't see Cheryl.

Cheryl missed the warm-up skate, but saw the face-off. Johnny won it, and the game was on.

Her feet soon tired of standing, and her cheeks got cold. Halfway through the second period Johnny still hadn't seen her. Or heard her, though she'd yelled herself hoarse over both of his team's goals.

Of course, everyone had been cheering then, too. The tying goal had nearly shaken the rafters.

Save your voice until he can hear you, dimwit.

The perfect opportunity came five minutes later when Johnny and an opponent were digging for the puck in the corner close to where Cheryl and Kathy stood. "Go, Johnny!" Cheryl yelled.

Johnny looked up. Underneath his sweat-soaked helmet she saw his eyes widen as he recognized her. Then his opponent stole the puck, and Johnny raced after him.

Too late. The RCMP team scored.

Cheryl winced. Kathy gave her shoulder an encouraging squeeze.

Johnny didn't even glance at Cheryl after that, concentrating ferociously on the puck. She couldn't blame him. Cheryl stared blindly at the stands across the ice.

She shouldn't have let Kathy talk her into coming to the game. She was the last person Johnny would—

Her gaze lit on The Stranger.

He was standing across the rink and five rows up from them, but his gaze connected with Cheryl's as if they were standing three feet away.

Her arms broke out in gooseflesh, and her fingers pressed against the glass. She couldn't look away. She nudged Kathy, but then couldn't speak and Kathy returned to watching the game. The Stranger's dark eyes held her, pinned her, like a butterfly to a styrofoam pad.

She remembered. Crack-the-whip. The Stranger first in the stands, then moving closer, onto the ice. Through her. She'd screamed. Then the concussion.

The Stranger smiled, and the sight stole what little warmth there was from the arena, turning it as cold as the Arctic night outside.

Something bad is going to happen.

❄ ❄ ❄ ❄

Why was Cheryl here? Johnny didn't think she'd been to a game since she'd broken up with Minik. He avoided looking at her, but found himself showing off for her, skating faster, avoiding a defenceman and smoothly passing the puck to Evan farther down the ice. Close to where Cheryl was sitting.

Thump! An RCMP player checked Evan into the boards, pressing his helmeted face hard against the glass. It was a hard check; Evan slid down onto the ice.

The puck was still loose in the corner, and the RCMP player was digging madly for it around Evan's body. Johnny rushed in to challenge him and saw that, instead of scrambling to his feet, Evan was still lying on the ice. Johnny forgot about the puck. Was Evan just stunned or more badly hurt? His helmet was still on, a good sign.

Johnny turned his skate sideways in the smooth braking motion that had been trained into him since Peewees—

—and tripped over a hidden crack in the ice.

His arms flailed, and his feet shot out from under him. "No!" he screamed as the sharpened blade of his skate sliced into his brother's throat.

CHAPTER 14

-35 °C (-31 °F)

BLOOD SPURTED FROM EVAN'S THROAT, staining the artificial ice pink. The crowd fell silent, their expressions horrified.

He lost blood fast. Pumped from the adrenaline of the game, Evan's pulse was beating twice every second.

"Evan!" Johnny screamed, falling to his knees by his unconscious brother.

Beside Cheryl, Kathy pressed against the glass, sobbing, beating frantically at the partition, unable to get to Evan. She turned and pushed her way along the boards until she reached a spot she could climb over.

A nurse in the stands bulldozed her way down onto the ice, and everyone with a cell phone called for an ambulance, but Cheryl doubted it would get there in time. So much blood...

Cheryl averted her gaze from the red, slick sight of it and saw Johnny. Everyone else was watching Evan. Only she was watching Johnny.

He kept shaking his head. Shock bleached his face, making his freckles stand out. Cheryl didn't know Evan that well, but—Oh, God—Johnny. She hurt for him. He was dying out there, too. Down on his knees, shoulders slumped, crushed down onto the ice by the hand of guilt. He had done this. His skate had cut his brother's throat.

"No, Johnny," Cheryl said, her voice choked. "It wasn't your fault." But he didn't hear her.

The nurse pushed him out of the way. Johnny stared as she bent over Evan's body, unwound her scarf and pressed it against the wound. Kathy tore off her jacket and laid it over top of Evan's torso to keep him warm.

The Stranger, who had been up in the stands only seconds ago, was suddenly on the ice beside Johnny.

"It hurts, doesn't it, Johnny?" The Stranger's cold voice held no compassion.

"Yes." Johnny kept staring at Evan. The nurse's white scarf soaked through within seconds, saturated with blood.

"I can make it stop, Johnny. I can take the hurt away. Just like I did last time."

Two paramedics from the ambulance burst into the arena and hurried toward the pitiful shape on the ice that was Evan.

"Do you want me to stop the pain, Johnny?" The Stranger asked.

Johnny looked up, and the raw pain and guilt on his face drove a stake into Cheryl's heart. "Yes, yes! *Anything,* only make it stop! Please, Frost."

The Stranger—Frost?—looked as if he were trying to smile, but only bared his teeth. He reached out with one white misshapen finger and touched Johnny's cheek *through* the clear plastic of his hockey mask.

Johnny's tears halted. His expression smoothed over, and the grief evaporated from his face. He straightened and actually picked up his hockey stick.

Only a moment had passed. The paramedics had put an oxygen mask over Evan's face and stuck two IV's in his arms. They transferred him first to a backboard and then a stretcher, keeping his head immobile with two orange blocks.

In a blink The Stranger, the man Johnny had called Frost, vanished as the paramedics carried Evan out of the arena. Kathy and the nurse went with them, the nurse still applying pressure with her blood-soaked scarf. The fringed end trailed along the ice.

Cheryl snapped out of the paralysis that had gripped her when she saw The Stranger. Desperate to get to Johnny, Cheryl shoved her way through a knot of onlookers and onto the ice through the Zamboni entrance.

"Johnny!" Cheryl ran up to him, but his cool expression stopped her just short of touching him. Later she regretted that. She should have hugged him, broken through to him somehow. "Come on. I'll take you to the hospital." She didn't have a license, but Johnny had let her drive his car a couple of times.

Johnny resisted her urging. "The hospital? I can't go there. The game's not over yet."

A terrible roaring sounded in Cheryl's ears. "What about Evan?" Minik and Brendan, who had skated over, added their protests.

Johnny looked unconcerned. "Evan will be fine. Head wounds always look worse than they actually are."

Evan didn't have a head wound; he had a cut throat. Cheryl exchanged glances with his horrified friends.

"He must be in shock." Brendan tried to excuse Johnny.

Cheryl didn't believe it. She noticed a small white patch on his face where The Stranger had touched him. Frostbite.

"Yeah, that's probably why they took him to the hospital," Johnny said, misunderstanding. "Cheryl, you shouldn't be out here on the ice. As soon as they clean up, the game will start again." He skated towards the bench.

Clean up. Cheryl glanced at the puddle of blood on the ice and doubted anyone would want to keep playing. Except Johnny. "He's in denial," she said firmly to Minik and Brendan. "You're going to have to help me get him to the hospital. Brendan, you get Evan's car keys. Minik, you help me handle Johnny."

When the stands emptied, Cheryl managed to persuade Johnny there wasn't going to be any more hockey that night, but he seemed exasperated by her insistence that he go to the hospital, as if she were being unreasonable. He balked again when Minik brought his boots out of the dressing room. He wanted to change out of his uniform not just his skates.

Cheryl grabbed his ear and twisted. "We don't have time. You're coming with me now."

"Hey," Johnny protested, sounding wounded, but he followed her out to the car and got in the back seat between her and Brendan.

The car didn't want to start. It whined and shuddered and died. Turned over, started to catch—and died. Minik floored it, roaring the engine to give it a chance to warm up. Once it had been running for five minutes, he started to back it out of the parking spot. It died again. Minik swore and tried again.

The trip to the hospital took three times as long as it should have because the car died every few blocks, despite Minik's careful coaxing. Cheryl wanted to scream at Minik, but knew he was doing as best as he could.

Johnny seemed in good spirits, talking about the hockey game and reliving his goal and assist. Every word he said made Cheryl feel colder. She interrupted. "Who was that man with you on the ice? The one you called Frost."

Johnny flinched, but in the next second his expression smoothed over. "Nobody. Just someone from the crowd."

"You're lying," Cheryl said, but just then they reached the parking lot of the Baffin Regional Hospital.

She got out of the car, but Johnny refused to budge. "Evan's fine. He'll be embarrassed if I go in after him. It was just a nick. You go if you want." He started to hum along with the radio.

How could he hum?

Cheryl considered grabbing him by the ear again, but decided not to. She didn't want the whole town to see him being led that way. "Okay, you stay in the car. I'll go in and check on Evan's condition." Find out if he was dead or not.

Minik and Brendan got out with her, but joined the line-up in the hall to donate blood while Cheryl pushed her way through to the orange-striped waiting room where Kathy was standing. Kathy looked white and strained, caught between hope and fear. Kathy shook her head at Cheryl's silent question. There was no news.

Two minutes after Cheryl got there, the Vander Zees dashed in. "Is Evan okay?" Pat Vander Zee asked.

Kathy burst into tears. Pat Vander Zee sat by her while her husband Dan paced. He looked surprised when he noticed Cheryl. "What are you doing here?"

"I was standing with Kathy when it happened..." she trailed off, but Johnny's uncle didn't seem to require any further explanation.

"Where's Johnny?" he asked.

Sitting in the car, humming. "He wouldn't come in. It was his skate that cut Evan's throat, and he feels guilty. He's in shock, not acting rationally." The explanation sounded lame to her, but Dan Vander Zee just nodded, his whole mind worried about Evan.

The doctor came out to see them.

As soon as he appeared, Pat Vander Zee was on her feet. "Is he all right? Is he—?"

The doctor responded with a calm summary. "Evan's in serious condition, but we've stabilized him. His carotid artery was severed, and he has a mild concussion. We've put in a breathing tube to allow him air, and we've sedated him. A medevac team will be at the airport to pick him up in twenty minutes. They'll fly him to Ottawa. He's going to need surgery—"

"Will he live?" Pat Vander Zee asked the question uppermost in everyone's minds.

"His chances are fair to good. The length of the flight worries me, but Evan's strong and healthy." The doctor smiled reassurance.

Cheryl didn't hear much after that. Her knees felt weak. He wasn't dead.

"Can we see him?" Kathy asked tearfully.

The doctor led the way to the ambulance bay. Cheryl followed, but, after one glimpse of Evan's open-eyed, vacant stare, returned to the waiting room. She debated going back out to the car to tell Johnny, but decided to wait. She didn't know if she could face his cheerful humming right now.

They waited in painful silence for the medevac team to arrive at the airport. The waiting room had a TV and stacks of magazines, but no one touched them.

When they took Evan away in an ambulance to the airport, his condition still stable, Cheryl let out a sigh of relief. She would be able to tell Johnny that Evan was alive. Johnny hadn't killed his own brother.

Was the humming he'd being doing in the car an act, a defence mechanism to keep his mind from acknowledging the terrible truth of what had happened? Or did he simply not care? In her mind she replayed the terrible change that had come over him when The Stranger touched him. The coldness.

"Do you want me to stop the pain, Johnny?"

Who was he that his fingers could pass through plastic? What had he done to Johnny?

Cheryl started to leave, anxious to tell Johnny the good news, but halted when she heard Pat Vander Zee mutter, "That damn ice.

Why is it always ice with their family? First Ned and Elizabeth, and now Evan."

"What do you mean? Who are Ned and Elizabeth?" Cheryl asked urgently.

Pat Vander Zee looked surprised. "You don't know? Ned and Elizabeth were the boys' parents. They were driving the boys to a hockey tournament, and their car skidded on the ice."

Glare ice. Horizon whirling—

"The car went onto a pond, and the ice gave way."

CRACK, CRACK, CRACK! Cold water pouring in through the floorboards—

"The car flooded. If that happens, you're supposed to roll down the windows before you sink so you can swim out, or wait until the water has risen high enough that the pressure on both sides is equalized. But, of course, poor Elizabeth didn't know that. She opened the door and let the water in."

A black wall of water smashed her against the steering wheel—

"Ned got Johnny out, God only knows how, but drowned going back for Evan and Elizabeth. Evan was trapped under the ice for ten minutes, but they managed to resuscitate him."

The little boy screamed as water rushed into his nose and mouth, filling them—

Oh, God. It hadn't been a story at all. Out on the ice Cheryl had asked Johnny to tell her about his parents, but when he had she hadn't been listening. She'd thought it was just a story, but Johnny had actually lived through that nightmare. He was the little boy.

Only in his story Johnny had changed the ending. The boy's parents and brother had been saved, but not himself. When Kathy had asked why he hadn't written a happy ending, he'd said: *"The little brat caused the accident. He deserved to die."*

But Johnny had only distracted his father for a second. It had been an accident. No one's fault.

And now Johnny thought he'd killed Evan, too.

Cheryl started to run through the hospital corridors, desperate to get to Johnny. Bits and scraps of conversation whirled in her brain, fitting together like a jigsaw puzzle.

The Stranger: *"I can take the hurt away, Johnny. Just like I did last time."*

Last time when his parents died by ice and cold.

The polar bear they'd confronted while The Stranger smiled, the snowmobile accident, the sea ice cracking underfoot, her concussion and now Evan. All ice and cold.

She burst out of the hospital doors and ran for the parking lot, heedless of the ice, of the cold air that caught and stalled in her lungs.

She kept remembering Johnny asking her on the phone if she trusted him and how brutally she'd answered him. He'd been trying to tell her about The Stranger and she'd failed him. She'd failed Johnny.

And again now. She reached the spot where they'd left the car, but it was gone. Johnny was gone.

She saw again the white patch of frostbite on Johnny's cheek where The Stranger had touched him. The Stranger with his silver hair and cold dark eyes.

Johnny had called him Frost, but frost wasn't a last name, she suddenly understood. It was a description. The Stranger *was* frost, and Frost wasn't human. He was something else entirely.

❄ ❄ ❄ ❄

A wall of glass separated Johnny from the rest of the world. Everyone looked strange through the glass, distorted. The people in the car had wanted him to go inside the hospital, but Johnny hadn't wanted to go.

He didn't need to go inside to know that Evan was dead.

Evan...

A crack appeared in the glass, then just as quickly smoothed over. The glass grew thicker. No, not glass. Ice. A layer of ice, encasing him on all sides.

The people had talked some more and then got out of the car.

Go to the airbase, Frost's voice said when he could no longer see them.

Johnny moved into the driver's seat and put the car in reverse. He felt absolutely nothing.

CHAPTER 15

-35 °C (-31 °F)

KATHY LEFT THE HOSPITAL in a daze of fear and hope.

Minik caught her arm in the lobby, his face anxious. "How—?"

She spared him from having to ask the question. "Evan was alive when they put him on the plane. The doctor said his chances were fair to good."

Minik looked relieved, but Kathy couldn't help but think that 'fair to good' wasn't the same thing as 'good'. What if—? Blinking back tears, she walked past Minik outside into the cold parking lot, then stopped. She'd driven here in the ambulance.

"Need a ride?" Minik asked.

Kathy nodded gratefully, and Minik bullied one of his many cousins into lending him his snowmobile. She piled on behind Minik, her mind following the plane and Evan. She didn't really rouse until they reached the gate to the airbase.

A dull warning rang in the back of her head when the snowmobile's headlights revealed that the gatehouse guard was standing straight up instead of slumped in his chair, and the gate arm stayed in the down position. The exhaustion and worry she had been feeling for Evan sharpened into new anxiety.

The base was on alert.

"Just let me off here," she told Minik. "I'll walk the rest of the way."

"Are you sure? It's pretty cold," Minik said.

"I need to clear my head," Kathy told him. An alert was base business, and she didn't want to alarm Minik. "Thanks for the ride."

Minik still looked doubtful, but complied. Kathy walked towards the lighted gatehouse, hunching deeper into her long winter coat.

"Miss O'Dwyer?" The gatehouse guard looked relieved to see her.

Kathy attempted to smile, then gave it up as a lost cause. She wanted to ask him about the alert at the base—what was happening?—but she knew better. Major O'Dwyer's daughter or not, she was still a civilian. If the guard told her, he might get in trouble for it.

She risked a less important question. "How long?"

"An hour," he murmured.

An hour was too soon to know if it was the real thing or just a drill. Kathy prayed the alert wasn't anything serious. Not a terrorist attack, not a war.

She wondered if one of the radars in the North Warning System had picked something up. Kathy listened for the scream of jets in the air, but, to her relief, didn't hear any. Iqaluit Air Base was one of NORAD's Forward Operating Locations. If something came up on the radar, Canadian CF-18s would be launched to intercept and identify approaching enemy aircraft.

But by now the jets might already be in the air. Kathy had to bite her lip to keep from asking the guard. It wasn't fair to put him in such an awkward position.

The gatehouse soldier's acne-pocked face was familiar to Kathy, but she didn't know his name. He looked uneasy, a fact which she had attributed to the alert, but his next words disabused her.

"Say, I need you to get your boyfriend off the base. I waved him through about five minutes before the alert started. I didn't realize you weren't at home—I got a busy signal when I called..."

But Evan was being flown to Ottawa, he couldn't be here. It took Kathy's clogged mind a long moment to realize the guard had probably mistaken Johnny for Evan.

He hadn't been at the hospital. Kathy hadn't thought of it at the time, but he hadn't been there. She had seen Cheryl, but not Johnny.

What on earth was Johnny doing here? Kathy decided she didn't care. She didn't have the energy to deal with Johnny just now. She'd send him to Cheryl.

Kathy left the guard in his warm little booth and began the four-block walk home in the dark. Her feet dragged. God, she was tired. The waiting room had been very tense, and the ambulance that took Evan to the airport to meet the medevac team had brought only a little relief. Evan could still die. The thought brought on a hitching sob, and tears froze in her eyelashes.

And now the alert on top of everything else. She wished fervently that her mother wasn't on a Christmas shopping trip to Montreal. Kathy had never been through an alert alone. Usually, after her father kissed them goodbye—as per protocol he never said there was a base alert, but a sudden phone call in the middle of the night and a kiss goodbye were good clues—she and her mother would stay up all night playing Monopoly and watching CNN. Waiting for either her father to come home or for the TV to give them some clue what was going on.

She would call her mom, Kathy decided, the second she got inside. But then the phone line would be tied up, if there was news about Evan....

Kathy's cheeks were stinging when she reached her house and saw Johnny and Evan's old car parked out front.

Johnny got out of the car when he saw her come up. "Hi, Kathy. I rang the bell, but your dad doesn't seem to be home."

His casualness made Kathy stop short, but she didn't know what to say. Johnny, I'm so sorry, or, Why didn't you come to the hospital? The slap of the wind made up her mind for her. It was too cold to stand outside a moment more than necessary. Wordlessly, she unlocked the door and went inside. Johnny followed.

Kathy began to peel off her layers of winter clothes. Johnny, as usual, looked perfectly comfortable in a sweater and short winter jacket with no toque and his bare hands stuck in his pockets. While they were dating, she'd nagged him about dressing more warmly. Today she didn't say a word. Matters were more serious than that.

Johnny didn't seem to realize they were chatting. "Is something going on at the base here? Everyone seems extra busy."

Kathy ignored his frivolousness and picked Question Number Two. "Why didn't you come to the hospital?"

Johnny shrugged. "There was no need."

Kathy felt her temper heat—Evan was his brother—but curbed herself. In her mind, she saw again Johnny's skate slicing open Evan's tender throat. Johnny must be suffering the tortures of the damned right now—though he was hiding it, as always. "Everyone knows that it was an accident. Nobody blames you, Johnny."

"Nobody?" Johnny's eyes had the glassy look of a wounded animal who knows it is dying. "I wouldn't say nobody blames me. I blame me."

"It wasn't your fault. You didn't—"

"Then who did, Kathy? My skate cut him. I've never slipped before. Never. But tonight, whoosh! Blood like a fountain. I killed my brother."

His words were like a hammer striking bone. Kathy inhaled sharply. "Don't say that! Evan's not dead. He's alive." Or he had been when they put him aboard the plane...

Johnny's face contorted once, before becoming blank. "Don't lie to me. I saw the blood. He's dead."

Kathy took a deep breath. "I know the blood looked bad, but they replaced it. You weren't there, Johnny. I was at the hospital. I know. Believe me. *Evan was alive when they put him on the plane.* The doctor said his chances were fair to good."

Johnny refused to listen. His face stayed cold and blank, punishing himself for Evan's death by not allowing himself to feel. "I'm the only one left of my family. The only one left alive."

"That's not true," Kathy protested. "Even if Evan does die—which he won't—you wouldn't be alone. You have your aunt and uncle." She paused. "You should have come inside the hospital, Johnny. The Vander Zees need you."

He focused on her again. "They've never needed me. Uncle Dan took us in out of love for my father, his brother, not for Evan and me. Aunt Pat never wanted to have children. She's a decent woman, and she's treated us well, but we were never a family. She and Uncle Dan are a family, a self-sufficient unit. They don't need me." His voice was flat.

Kathy remembered how upset Pat Vander Zee had been when Johnny had refused his favourite dessert. And there had certainly been genuine shock and concern on Pat's face at the hospital. Maybe it hadn't been the wild grief of a mother, but maybe she just wasn't the type of woman to break down in public and would cry buckets when she got home. "You don't know that," Kathy said. "Sometimes a crisis can bring a family together. You should go home. Your uncle must be worried sick about you."

Johnny shook his head. "I'm not going home."

"You have to go home sometime, Johnny," Kathy said gently. "You can't stay here. The gate guard shouldn't have let you in."

"I guess I'd better go then," Johnny said.

His swift agreement made uneasiness prowl down Kathy's spine. "Are you sure you're okay? I mean, okay enough to drive?"

"Why wouldn't I be okay?" Johnny asked tonelessly. "My throat wasn't cut; Evan's was. I killed him."

"He's not dead." Kathy took another deep breath. "Do you want me to drive you?"

Johnny shook his head and left.

Kathy frowned, watching him start his car. He looked fine, and he'd obviously driven here without problem, but it felt wrong to leave him alone after what had happened to Evan.

The truth was, Kathy acknowledged, she didn't want to be alone herself. When she'd asked to be driven home, she'd thought her dad would be here to make her cocoa and hug her.

The wind slammed the door shut, and in the kitchen the telephone started to ring.

Kathy kicked off her boots and ran for the phone. "Mom?"

"Sorry, no, this is Cheryl. Look, do you know where Johnny is? It's very important that I talk to him."

"He just left," Kathy said. She could see his taillights disappearing through the kitchen window.

"Where did he go?" Cheryl's voice was clipped, urgent.

"Home, I think." Even as Kathy said the words she doubted them. Johnny hadn't actually said he would go home, just that he would leave.

"I'll try the Vander Zees' again, then," Cheryl said. "Bye."

"Wait!" Kathy was startled to find herself gripping the phone with white knuckles.

"What?" Cheryl asked.

"I'm not sure Johnny went home. Why did you need to talk to him?" Kathy's mind raced ahead. "You don't think he's suicidal, do you?" Damn it, she shouldn't have let him leave! Never mind the base alert, her dad would have understood.

Cheryl's hesitation before answering tightened Kathy's nerves another notch.

"No. Not suicidal. But I have a very bad feeling about all this. I have to find Johnny."

"Why? Tell me," Kathy demanded rawly. "I'm in this, too."

"I think I know why Johnny's been acting so strangely," Cheryl said. And told her, while outside Kathy heard the telltale scream of jets launching into the air.

❄ ❄ ❄ ❄

The ice around his heart had cracked slightly while he talked to Kathy, but as soon as Johnny went out the door it grew thick again.

Still, he was grateful when, after only driving one block, Frost's icy voice in his head told him to park the car. He didn't want to go home yet. Home where Aunt Pat and Uncle Dan might be, where Evan never would be again—

Ice.

Walk to the gray building, Frost commanded.

Johnny got out of the car and walked toward the gray building. He thought it might be the one Kathy had pointed out on one of their runs as the armoury.

What did Frost want with the armoury? Johnny wondered vaguely. A machine gun?

Oh. Frost's bomb. This was where he meant to get the missing explosives.

Go inside.

Johnny could have stopped walking, but it hardly seemed worth it. There were two guards outside. They would stop him soon enough. Maybe he would even go to prison.

Prison was where he belonged for killing his—

Ice.

A wind sprang up, blowing loose snow. Tiny ice spicules stung Johnny's face. The guards pulled their hoods further down and turned so their faces were out of the wind.

Johnny walked right past them, unseen.

He reached a chainlink fence, seven feet high and topped with barbed wire. It looked like a good way to get himself killed. Johnny put the toe of his boot into one of the links and grabbed the chainlink with both hands. Almost academically he wondered if it would be electrified...

Instead the wire links disintegrated in his hands, made brittle by extreme cold. By Frost. They fell on the sidewalk with a tinging sound.

Johnny walked through the fence and on towards the armoury. There would be more guards inside to stop him, or the ones outside would patrol to warm up and notice the big hole in their fence.

The lock on the armoury was electronic and a video camera swung back and forth, panning the doorway. Johnny watched to see how Frost was going to handle this one.

Within seconds on his approach, needles of frost covered the camera's lens.

Open the door.

Johnny pushed on it, and the electronic card lock cracked and fell off. The door opened easily.

A single clerk sat inside. He came to his feet in a rush when Johnny entered, then he inexplicably slipped. At first Johnny didn't understand why and then he saw the patch of ice where no ice should be. Indoors. The man didn't get up. A spreading pool of blood formed by his head.

Johnny hesitated. The blood reminded him of Evan—

Ice.

Johnny went past the body into the armoury. It looked like no one was going to stop him, after all.

CHAPTER 16

-25 °C (-13 °F)

CHERYL COULD HEAR RAVEN laughing in the harsh wind.

Johnny had not gone home. In the hour since he had left the airbase Johnny had not gone to Minik's or Brendan's or the home of any of the other half-dozen hockey players Cheryl had phoned. She had made Minik and Brendan promise to call her if Johnny showed up, but the phone had been frustratingly silent.

Pat Vander Zee had also promised to call and had extracted the same promise in return. "If you get hold of him, be sure to tell him we've booked him on a 6 a.m. flight to Ottawa tomorrow. Tell him to get his butt home now." Pat's voice crackled with tension.

Cheryl didn't think Johnny had any intention of flying to Ottawa. According to Kathy, he was over his denial and now believed Evan was dead.

Cheryl prayed that Evan would live. Not just for Evan's sake, but for Johnny's.

Where could Johnny be? Images of Johnny dripping icicles, frozen stiff in his inadequate winter clothes, flitted through her mind like ghosts.

She stared at the phone some more, but it remained silent.

Finally, at two a.m. the phone rang. Cheryl snatched it up. "Johnny?" But it was Pat Vander Zee. She gave Cheryl the news on Evan: he had survived the flight and would undergo surgery in the morning. "Johnny's still not back, damn him. Dan's worried sick—he shouldn't have to deal with one of Johnny's stunts on top of everything else. I've finally persuaded Dan to go to bed, and I'm going to follow him soon. When Johnny comes in, I'll tell him to call you." Pat paused. "Try to get some sleep. I'm sure he's fine."

Cheryl's body ached with fatigue, and her eyes felt gritty, but she didn't think she would be able to sleep. She would be too worried about missing a phone call, or Johnny's knock on the door.

Her grandfather came into the kitchen and laid an arthritic hand on her shoulder. "Go to sleep. I will listen for your phone."

It was a major concession. Her grandfather considered the phone to be a waste of time and would often listen to over twenty rings while slowly tying off a bit of harness before getting up to answer it.

"Thank you." Cheryl got up and went down to the bedroom she shared with her aunt. She fell into her bed and didn't move until her grandfather woke her up six hours later.

"A woman to talk to you," he said in Inuktitut.

Cheryl dragged herself to the kitchen. The phone was lying off the hook on the table. She picked it up. "Hello?"

"Cheryl? Pat Vander Zee here," a voice said crisply. "I just called to let you know Johnny has returned. The car's parked out front. I'm afraid I went back to bed after Dan left for his flight, and I didn't hear it. I didn't wake up until the dog started howling."

"Is Johnny there?" Cheryl spoke around a tongue that felt as dry and fuzzy as a cotton blanket. "Can I talk to him?" She needed to talk to him, get through to him somehow. Tell him she knew who The Stranger really was, that Johnny didn't have to face him alone anymore.

Pat had paused for too long. "I assumed Johnny was in his bedroom, but let me check."

A click on the line. While on hold, Cheryl yawned repeatedly and widened her eyes, trying to wake up. She looked at a clock. 8:35 a.m.

It was dark outside, dawn still forty-five minutes away.

Pat Vander Zee picked up the phone again. "He's not in his room. It doesn't look like he's been inside at all—there's no snow melting in the porch. It's definitely the right car—hold on a minute, I think I hear something."

Cheryl held on.

"It's the snowmobile." Pat sounded angry. "He's going out on the snowmobile. And I can't get there fast enough on crutches to stop him." She hung up.

Cheryl put the receiver down more slowly on her end. The snowmobile. What had Johnny been doing all night and where was he going now?

Somewhere he couldn't go by car.

Out onto the snow and ice, home of Frost.

For a moment, Cheryl teetered on the edge of remembering something, something Johnny had said living in an ice epoch that she had disregarded as unimportant, not listening.... Then the wisp of memory faded. She phoned Kathy.

The O'Dwyers must have had caller i.d. because Kathy didn't bother to say hello. "Any news?" she demanded.

"Johnny returned the car, but left in the snowmobile." Determination crystallized in Cheryl's mind. "I'm going after him."

"I'm coming, too," Kathy said at once.

"Evan's in surgery this morning. Don't you want to wait and find out how he does?"

"Yes," Kathy admitted. "But I can't do anything to help Evan now. Evan would want us to go after Johnny and make sure he doesn't do anything... foolish. Besides, the base is already so tense, every fighter jet taking off makes me want to scream. Since I can't fly, I need to get away from here."

"Get away from what?"

"Haven't you heard the news?" Kathy asked in disbelief. "North Korea has invaded South Korea. The U.S. is sending in troops and North Korea is threatening to use its nukes if it does."

Cheryl had no time for international news today. "I'm leaving in ten minutes. If you're not here, too bad." She hung up.

She looked up to see her grandfather calmly drinking the last of his tea. "I'll harness the dogs," he said.

Cheryl opened her mouth to protest, then shut it. She had intended to phone Minik and borrow his snowmobile, but Grandfather was right, the dogs would be best.

A snowmobile could travel distances much faster than a dogsled, but it was a machine. In cold weather the best vehicle might refuse to start. She remembered the way Johnny's car had kept stalling on the trip to the hospital. Had Frost been responsible for that? If they took a snowmobile, Frost might wait until they were a mile out of town and then kill the motor.

If she asked them to, the dogs would run until they fell down and died.

Cheryl dressed as warmly as possible. Thick socks and kamiks trimmed with Arctic fox fur. Long underwear, corduroy pants and ski-pants. Long-sleeved shirt, turtleneck sweater and a long parka with a hood with a fur ruff to protect her face from the wind. Balaclava. Gloves and lined sealskin mitts.

Once she started out on the trail she would have to take off some of the layers, but it would all be there to put back on if the weather turned nasty.

If Frost made the weather turn nasty.

After a little thought, Cheryl decided to pack a first aid kit and some food as well.

She went outside and saw that her grandfather had the sled upside-down and was rubbing boiling water onto the runners with a polar bear hide. Once the runners were iced up they would slide better on the tundra.

Cheryl helped her grandfather hitch the seven dogs to the gang-line. The huskies were all excited. They loved to run and, with a double-layer of fur and feet like small snowshoes, cold and snow didn't bother them.

Kathy arrived two minutes later in a jeep. She was dressed just as warmly as Cheryl, although her clothes all sported brand names and looked liked they'd been designed by scientists.

"Are you nuts?" Kathy asked when she saw the dogs. "Johnny has a snowmobile. Dogs are way too slow."

Cheryl didn't argue, just took the dogs out of the yard and headed for Johnny's house. They could pick up the trail of the snowmobile there.

Kathy passed her in the jeep moments later.

Shadow, the lead dog, started out at a trot, his black head held at an alert angle. Lead dogs were always the smartest and fastest. In a race they were the ones who wanted to win just as much as the driver. A pair of point dogs followed, who would help steer the team. Then the steady swing dogs, and, last of all, the wheel dogs, who were the largest and strongest and helped control the sled.

At the Vander Zees' place Samwise started howling as soon as they entered the yard. Cheryl was used to dogs howling—huskies were so closely related to wolves that they couldn't bark—but Samwise sounded desolate. Her tension kicked up another notch. Johnny was in trouble; she wasn't imagining things. Cheryl waved to Pat Vander Zee in the window, but didn't bother to go in, just headed straight for Johnny's dog.

Kathy's jeep was already parked, slantwise, by the house. Moments later Kathy burst out the door and roared off on Evan's snowmobile while Cheryl untied Samwise.

She held his furry head in her mittened hands for a moment, looking deep into his blue eyes. "Go find Johnny," she told him. "He needs us."

Samwise nuzzled her palms in seeming agreement. Cheryl hoped the journey wouldn't be too hard on the seven-month-old pup. He was certainly eager to go. As soon as she released him, Samwise took off at a run, looking back as if urging them to follow.

Shadow looked to Cheryl, waiting for her to give the command. Once she did Shadow bent his head, dug in and pulled. Sled runners squeaked on the snow. Shadow loved to race—he'd won the endurance race during Iqaluit's Toonik Tyme festival last April.

Ten minutes later Cheryl and the dogs reached the edge of town—and drew even with Kathy, who was trying to restart the stalled snowmobile.

"The engine just stopped," Kathy fumed as she abandoned the snowmobile and jumped on board. "I don't understand it. The engine was nicely warmed up and running smoothly. Evan and I have ridden this machine in twenty below weather before, no problem."

"If you don't understand by now, maybe you shouldn't come," Cheryl said, exasperated.

"What do you mean by that?" Underneath her navy blue balaclava, Kathy sounded angry.

"Our enemy is Frost," Cheryl said. "He doesn't want us to get to Johnny. Tonight is the solstice. The longest night of the year. Frost's power is probably at its peak."

❄ ❄ ❄ ❄

Johnny had done everything Frost wanted him to do, and now even Frost had gone away. No cold presence remained in his mind. Johnny was alone. No people anywhere. At first he'd been glad to get on his snowmobile and leave Iqaluit because of the bomb in his backpack, but now the bomb barely seemed to matter. Strange that he'd always hated being alone. Right now it was a relief.

The damn dog had wanted to go with him. Somehow that had almost brought tears to his eyes; the tears that hadn't come for Evan came when Samwise howled mournfully. *Go away, I'm trying to save you,* he'd told the dog, because, of course, he had a bomb. And Frost wanted him to set it off somewhere.

It didn't matter where as long as nobody but Johnny was hurt. In town Cheryl and Aunt Pat could be hurt. Not Evan, though. Evan was beyond—

Ice.

The familiar curtain of snow fell on Johnny's mind, muffling his thoughts and freezing his pain.

He continued across the tundra, mind empty.

CHAPTER 17

-25 °C (-13 °F)

"I'M NOT GOING TO LET FROST HAVE JOHNNY," Cheryl said. "In order to catch up, we're going to have to travel fast. Have you ever driven a team?"

Kathy shook her head.

"If we both ride on the sled, we'll slow the dogs too much. We'll have to jump off and run a lot," Cheryl warned. "Are you up for it?"

"Frost caused Evan's accident. I owe him for that," Kathy said.

Cheryl took that as a yes. "Watch me." She stepped off the back of the sled and began to run behind the dogs, keeping hold of the sled handles. "Your turn," she told Kathy and moved aside so that Kathy could jump down while she took a short rest.

The streetlights in town had made it fairly easy to pick up Johnny's trail, but as they rode farther out onto the tundra the track faded. Dawn was still fifteen minutes away, but the reflection of the moonlight on snow gave the world a ghostly radiance. Cheryl could see a little, but from here they would have to trust the dogs, Samwise and Shadow both.

Johnny, of course, wouldn't have suffered the same disadvantage. Snowmobiles had headlights. Dogsleds didn't.

Johnny had a head start and a faster method of transportation. The urgency of a race pounded inside Cheryl. *Hurry, hurry.*

She let the dogs have their heads, and Shadow lived up to her expectations. Johnny's snowmobile had packed the snow a little, making it easier for the dogs to run on.

"I can't see anything!" Kathy yelled, as she ran with Cheryl behind the dogsled.

"Me either!" Cheryl yelled back. The dogs were dim shapes ahead of her, as she followed the small spray of snow shot up by the sled's runners. She was sweating now and had to partially unzip her coat despite the freezing temperatures.

As they took turns running behind the sled and resting on its back runners, it became obvious that Kathy was in much better physical shape than Cheryl was, and Cheryl felt stupid at having implied Kathy wouldn't be able to hack it. Kathy's breaths were measured; Cheryl's were ragged pants. Still, Cheryl couldn't bear to ride on the sled for too long before she got off and ran again. *Hurry, hurry.*

She wondered if she should get off and let Kathy go ahead and intercept Johnny alone. But Cheryl didn't think Kathy could get through to him. After all, Kathy had had a chance last night and failed.

When sunrise found them at 9:20 a.m., Cheryl was relieved to see snowmobile tracks still stretching in front of them. No sign of Johnny, just the tracks going on and on.

"Where's he going?" Kathy asked, sending white puffs of vapor into the air with each word.

Cheryl shook her head. She didn't know, couldn't guess and hadn't the breath to talk anyway.

Ride and run, run and ride, ride and run.

The dogs were tireless. They loved to pull. Samwise, unencumbered, kept getting ahead, and Shadow kept wanting to go faster and catch him. Cheryl had to hold the team back, pace them.

At eleven a.m., they caught their first sight of Johnny.

"There he is!" Kathy pointed.

The small dot of the snowmobile was too far away to identify. They couldn't know if it was really Johnny or whether they'd crossed and started to follow somebody else's tracks in the dark. Still, Cheryl felt renewed determination flow into her tired legs. He wasn't going that fast. They could catch him.

"What's that?" Kathy asked a few minutes later.

Cheryl squinted into the snow glare. All she saw was white—and then she saw something more. What she'd thought was a snowy outcrop suddenly resolved into a wall of ice, very big and very far away.

"Wow," Kathy said, between breaths. "I didn't know there was a glacier so close to Iqaluit."

That's because there isn't, Cheryl thought, but didn't say. Her tongue felt tied up in her mouth, and Kathy wouldn't have understood anyway. Baffin Island had plenty of glaciers, but the nearest were some four hundred kilometers away, ice tongues flowing out from Penny Ice Cap.

Frost had done this. The hairs rose on the back of Cheryl's neck as she tried to grasp how much power it must have taken Frost to accomplish this. Glaciers were supposed to move, well, *glacially,* advancing in winter and retreating in summer, gaining or losing a few feet a year.

How much of the Penny Ice Cap had Frost had to deplete to push out a glacier so far? He was risking a lot and for what? Cheryl didn't know.

Over the next half hour, they came closer to the glacier, finally falling under its five-storey-high shadow.

The wall of ice at the foot of the glacier was fissured and dirty. And moving. Kathy hadn't noticed yet, but Cheryl was watching very closely and it was moving, if slowly.

"I've never seen one from up close before," Kathy said, awed. "Just a couple in the mountains, across a lake."

Cheryl wasn't awed; she was afraid. "There's an Inuit tale about a huge giant who sleeps in the far north," Cheryl said softly.

"A glacier?"

"Maybe. The giant is so large," Cheryl continued, "that his breath causes blizzards."

Ahead of them, Johnny got off his snowmobile and began to climb the glacier.

"What's he doing?" Kathy asked.

Cheryl didn't know, but Johnny's decision to go on foot gave them their first real chance to catch up with him. "Hurry," she gasped.

The dogs flew across the hard-packed tundra. Sunlight glinted off snow and ice, creating a glare that could blind.

"Oh my God," Kathy said suddenly. She stopped running.

The dogsled was fifteen feet ahead when Cheryl finally got the dogs stopped. She looked back and saw Kathy was still standing, staring at the glacier. "What are you doing? Get back on the sled!"

"Do you see that?" Kathy said instead, pointing.

Cheryl squinted. She saw nothing until Kathy walked up and turned her shoulders so Cheryl was facing the right direction. Cheryl saw a tangle of black metal jutting out of the snow, something she had mistaken for rock, but wasn't. "What is it?"

"Plane wreckage."

"I didn't know there had been a crash," Cheryl said indifferently. The moving dot that was Johnny had climbed to the top of the glacier. One of the bits of wreckage lay in his path. It was about the size of a snowmobile.

"I don't think it's a recent crash; it looks like the wind just uncovered it." For some reason Kathy still seemed excited. "I think he found it. The lost plane."

Cheryl didn't know what she was talking about. "Come on, we're wasting time."

Kathy resisted the pull on her arm. "No. This is important. My dad told a ghost story at Thanksgiving—Johnny was there—about a legendary lost plane that went down in a storm during the Cold War. They never found it."

"If a plane went down this close, how come the military never found it?" Cheryl asked skeptically. "You've got all those fancy radars, don't you?"

"The North Warning System, yes. But radar isn't perfect. Have you heard of stealth planes?"

Cheryl nodded impatiently.

"The reason they're called stealth planes is because they're built to deflect radar waves in such a way that they don't bounce back to the radar station," Kathy lectured. "They're also coated with a special radar-absorbing paint. According to what Dad said, they only caught the plane on radar intermittently. Two blips and then nothing. Stealth planes are very hard to track."

"So?"

"So that, my friend, is a stealth plane. Look over there. See the special gold transparent paint on the remains of the cockpit?"

"Maybe. Now can we get going again?"

"I suppose." Kathy sounded reluctant, but followed Cheryl back to where the dogs were waiting, tongue lolling.

"What I'd like to know is how Johnny knew the plane wreck was here. I mean, he led us straight to it."

"That's easy," Cheryl said. "Johnny couldn't have known it was here. Therefore, Frost must have led him here." And pushed out the glacier to meet him.

Kathy stopped dead again. Cheryl groaned. Couldn't she walk and talk at the same time?

"What if Frost made the plane crash in the first place?" Kathy asked. "Then covered it up with snow until today?"

"What would be the point?" Cheryl asked. "It's in twenty pieces; it's not like Johnny can fly it."

"No," Kathy said, "but look. Johnny's searching for something in the wreckage. What do you suppose that could be?"

"How should I—" Cheryl stopped. "Oh my God."

Kathy said it for her. "He's looking for a missile. A nuke." Some of Kathy's composure returned. "But the controls for that one will be with the plane. They'll be broken, and in Russian. He can't do anything with it."

"How sure are you of that?" Cheryl asked softly. "Are you sure there isn't any way for Frost to do it?"

Kathy thought for a minute, then shook her head. "No, I'm not sure. I remember reading somewhere that a small bomb exploded near a nuclear bomb might set off a sympathetic explosion. Ka-boom. And if Iqaluit Airbase is vaporized, chances are NORAD will assume it's North Korea's doing. They'll retaliate and the other side will do the same. China might get pulled in. More bombs. Nuclear war. Radiation. Death. Nuclear winter. The next ice age."

"An ice age." Cheryl remembered Johnny's ramblings out on the sea ice. She'd thought he was evading her question about his parents, but he'd been trying to tell her something important. "That's what Frost wants: permanent winter. We have to stop him." Cheryl started forward again.

"No. I have to go tell my dad this. We have to go back."

Cheryl didn't even consider it. "No."

"Look," Kathy said, "I care about Johnny, too, but if he's so far gone that he's playing with nukes then I seriously doubt he can be talked out of it. In fact, approaching him might make him set off his bomb sooner. We have to warn NORAD that if there is a nuclear explosion, it has nothing to do with North Korea. It's our duty."

The dot on the slope moved away from the first bit of wreckage and headed for another one, something shaped like a wing, searching.

"You can go back, if that's your duty," Cheryl said. "I have to get to Johnny."

For a second Kathy looked scared, then she straightened her shoulders. "Fine, then. I'll go by myself."

Kathy was a novice in the arctic. It was dangerous for her to travel alone, but Cheryl couldn't abandon Johnny. "Wait." Cheryl bent over the sled and took out a package. "Take some muktuk with you. Follow the path we made, don't take any shortcuts. It's local noon already. There are only about two hours of daylight left."

Kathy made a face. "I'll pass on the muktuk."

Cheryl shoved it into her hand. "Take it. Muktuk raises your body temperature; it'll keep you warm. Go." She gave Kathy a push and stepped onto the back of the sled.

On the ice, Johnny had reached the second piece of wreckage. "Let's go," she yelled to the dogs in Inuktitut, and they smoothly started running again. This time she stayed on the sled: it was more work for the dogs, but they could run faster than she could and speed was important now.

She reached Johnny's snowmobile at the foot of the glacier, and was unable to see Johnny any longer. His snowmobile had been unable to make it up the ice, but the slope was gentler than Cheryl had feared, a scree of tumbled ice and rocks. Shadow and the dogs were able to scramble up it. Cheryl had to get off the sled and help pull from above, but they made it. The sled got banged around, but none of the flexible rawhide strips her grandfather had used to bind the frame together broke and it was all still in one piece when they finally made it to the top of the glacier.

Johnny was standing by a piece of wreckage, still empty-handed. As she watched he headed for another scrap of twisted metal.

He was about one hundred and fifty feet away, and Cheryl saw for the first time that he wore skates.

Skates?

Cheryl blinked. It should have been impossible to skate on the uneven snow and ice surface, but, as she watched, the ice ahead of him spookily melted and refroze as smooth as a skating rink. Frost at work again.

Johnny skated forward with grace, but no hurry. If he knew Cheryl and the dogs were there, he gave no indication, even when Cheryl called, "Let's go!" to the dogs again.

He was closer to the piece of wreckage—what looked to be part one wing and some fuselage—than Cheryl was to him. "Faster," she called to the dogs. Samwise bounded ahead, eager to reach his master.

Bumps and cracks in the glacier's surface made the sled bounce, and the dogs' feet slipped and slid. She saw a smear of blood on the snow and wished she'd taken the time to put booties on the dogs.

Johnny disappeared briefly under the tipped-up wing, then re-emerged. While Cheryl was still fifty feet away he shrugged out of his backpack and set it down by his feet.

Samwise loped up to Johnny, wagging his tail as if overjoyed at having found his human.

Johnny ignored the husky.

He wasn't going to be able to ignore her. "Johnny," she called.

"Cheryl." Johnny looked unsurprised. He unzipped his backpack. "Stay back! Nothing you can say will change my mind."

"Not even that Evan's alive? He went into surgery this morning. Your aunt should have word on his progress soon."

"Evan's dead," Johnny said flatly. He pulled a clock and some wires out of his backpack. Then he pulled out a white block of something Cheryl suspected was plastique. Explosive.

"He was alive at 8:30 this morning. Don't you think you should wait and see if he survives before you blow everything up?" Forty feet away.

For a moment she thought she'd won. Hope sparked in Johnny's eyes; he started to put down the bomb. Then the patch of frostbite on his face—Frost's mark—turned white and Johnny's eyes dulled. He shrugged.

"I don't care. I don't care about anything any more. Not you, not Evan, not hockey. I'm frozen inside, and I like it. I feel no pain. I'll never feel pain again."

"What about joy? In stopping the hurt, you'll stop the joy, too."

Johnny took off his gloves and began to set the clock on his homemade bomb. "Go away, Cheryl," he said without looking up. "You gave up on me a long time ago, remember?"

The words hit like blows. She had given up on him. "I'm sorry about that, Johnny. I was trying to protect myself from being hurt."

No response.

Thirty feet away now. Cheryl had no illusions about who would win if it came down to a contest of physical strength, but she didn't think it would. This was about emotional strength. If she got close enough to hug Johnny, she had a feeling he would break down and cry.

Cheryl brought out the big guns. "I know what happened to your parents, Johnny. I know that the story you wrote was true."

Johnny's hands paused.

"After the Year of the Three Funerals I wanted to die, too, it hurt so much. But the pain eased. And then I met you and I felt alive again."

"But it doesn't last." Johnny resumed wiring. "Joy never does. And then I'm alone again."

"Neither does pain," Cheryl said simply. "You say you're frozen, but you lie. If you were frozen, you wouldn't care. But you're in pain, and you want to stop the pain."

"I feel nothing." Johnny sounded angry.

"Oh yeah? Watch this." As the sled moved forward, Cheryl began to take off her winter clothing, first her balaclava and scarf, throwing them behind her. She tossed her sealskin mitts down onto the sled, then shed her woolen gloves. She pushed down her hood and unzipped her jacket. The cold air greedily sucked away the warmth her exercise had provided.

"What the hell are you doing?" Johnny demanded. He stopped working on the bomb.

She was only twenty feet away from him now, and her heart felt suddenly light. "What's the matter, Johnny? Are you worried about me freezing to death? I thought you said you didn't care."

"I don't." Johnny's face hardened, and he bent over the bomb again. Frost kept his gloveless fingers nimble in the cold. "Give up, Cheryl. You could take all your clothes off, and it wouldn't stop me."

"I love you." Cheryl said the words for the first time, and they didn't hurt at all. They didn't stick in her throat as she had expected: they rang across the glacier. She took off her coat entirely and shed it like a butterfly emerging from a cocoon. "I love you, Johnny Vander Zee, and I will never give up on you."

Johnny stared blindly away, and Cheryl saw tears on his face.

Shadow was only six feet away from him now, pulling smoothly. *Just a little farther.*

CRACK!

A crevasse suddenly yawned between Cheryl and the dogs, and Cheryl cried out as she and the dogsled plunged over the edge.

❄ ❄ ❄ ❄

"No!" Johnny screamed.

The ice encasing him shattered.

CHAPTER 18

-25 °C (-13 °F)

INSTINCTIVELY, CHERYL FLUNG out both arms to catch herself, but her fingers slipped off the ice. She banged elbows and shins against the crevasse walls, falling. Screaming.

She dropped ten feet in a heartbeat, then, purely by accident, her body jammed in the narrow crevasse, slowing her descent. The contents of the dogsled, the blankets, the food, tumbled past her. She didn't hear them hit bottom.

Choking back sobs, Cheryl pressed her back against one wall while her toes dug into the other—thank God she hadn't removed her boots along with her jacket earlier. The position put an incredible strain on her muscles.

But there was no floor beneath her, and the slightest relaxation of her muscles caused her to slip and inch or a foot further down.

Fifteen feet down and slipping.

Oh, God, oh, God, oh, God...

Cheryl dug her toes harder into the ice. She dared not try climbing. If she took one foot off the ice, she would fall.

Helplessly, she looked up. The dogsled frame had jammed much higher up and soon vanished from view, pulled out by the dog team. Cheryl stared at the ribbon of blue sky overhead. It was as out of reach as the moon.

Her shoulders and thigh muscles quivered.

Her hands were more or less free, but her bare fingers couldn't get any purchase on the slick surface, and she fell another two inches. The ice felt cold against her back, now protected only by her sweater and undershirt.

It wouldn't be long before her muscles gave out and she fell.

"Cheryl!" Johnny's head blocked off part of the sky. "Cheryl!"

"Here."

Johnny looked astonished when Cheryl waved weakly. He'd probably expected her to be lying at the bottom of the crevasse with a broken neck. It's what she would have expected. What still might happen.

"Are you all right?"

"Define 'all right'." Cheryl slipped another inch. Her thighs screamed in agony.

"Hang in there." Johnny's voice sounded strained. "I'll unhitch the sled and lower the gang-line to you."

"I'm not going anywhere," Cheryl said, to herself since Johnny had already disappeared. She pressed her back tighter to the cold ice.

Long, long moments later, Johnny lay flat on the ice and lowered the gang-line to her. It fell eight feet short, so he pulled it back up and double-knotted a couple tuglines onto it. This time it stopped only a foot above Cheryl's head. Within reach, if she stretched and didn't slip.

"Cheryl, grab it!"

She stretched upward as far as she could while still pressing with her back. The line dangled five inches above her fingertips. "I can't reach!" Even as she spoke, she slipped down another inch.

Johnny had wound the straps around his hand three times to give himself a good grip. He unwound a layer now, giving her four more inches. "That's the best I can do," Johnny yelled from above. "You're going to have to jump for it."

Cheryl hesitated. She was afraid. "I'll fall."

"Do it now, Cheryl, before you fall farther out of reach!" Johnny sounded frantic, no ice man now.

He was right, she knew he was right, but it took a moment to gather her courage and be sure her locked muscles would work when she wanted them to.

"On the count of three," Johnny yelled. "One, two—"

Cheryl dug in hard with her toes and pushed upward with all her remaining strength. She caught the end of the line, but her boot slipped a fraction of a second later, and her full weight hung from Johnny's arms.

He grunted, and Cheryl hastily scrambled back into her sitting-against-the-wall position, terrified that the knots would slip out and she would fall.

"I've got you," Johnny sounded elated. "The two lead dogs are still hitched up. I'll get them to help pull you out."

"Wait!" Cheryl yelled before he could disappear again. "What about the bomb? You have to disarm it."

"Forget about the bomb," Johnny said impatiently. "We're far enough away that it won't kill us."

He didn't know. "It's a nuke. We can't get out of range."

"What? No, it's not, it's just C4."

"No. Frost brought you here because there's a nuclear missile in the plane wreckage. Your bomb will set it off and start a war, maybe a world war. Frost wants to bring on another ice age."

Johnny swore. "Hold on!" He disappeared from view.

❄ ❄ ❄ ❄

Johnny was caught in a nightmare. He had to save Cheryl—she could fall at any second—but the bomb. Frost had to be stopped. He skated forward, but he'd only taken two steps when Frost appeared between him and the bomb.

"Leave the bomb alone, Johnny."

Johnny's cheek burned where Frost had touched him. Ice kept creeping up around him, trying to cut him off from the world again. But this time Johnny fought it. He held the image of Cheryl down in the crevasse in his mind. She needed him.

"It's time the human race became extinct," Frost went on, hideously reasonable. "For as long as the earth has existed, it has followed cycles—both seasonal ones and ones that are much longer. But that cycle is faltering, changing because of Man, *and I do not like it.* All the other animals change if the environment changes, but Man wants to control the environment, control the weather. Only if Man is gone will the natural order be restored."

The words almost made sense. *Ignore them,* Johnny told himself. *Think about Cheryl.* Cheryl was important.

"Out of my way." Johnny pushed past Frost and knelt by the timer. Ten minutes still on the clock. Good.

"Leave the bomb alone, Johnny, or the girl dies."

Johnny faltered. As soon as he stopped moving, a thin veneer of ice began to grow between him and the real world again.

Dead black eyes stared into his. "I hold her life in my hand."

Johnny shook off the sudden paralysis that had crept over him. "No. Cheryl says you've got a nuke. If the bomb goes off, she and I are both dead." Along with a lot more people. Johnny wasn't very clear on the exact range of a nuke, but he was guessing Iqaluit would be toast and a big chunk of the Arctic would turn into radioactive waste. Goodbye Nunavut.

"I can protect you," Frost said. "Entomb you both in the ice and wake you in a few hundred years when it's safe."

Johnny hesitated, trying to think through the coldness creeping into his heart. Trying to remember why Frost's offer was a bad idea. Cheryl was the important thing. And Cheryl wanted him to disarm the bomb. He reached for the clock again.

"Then she dies," Frost said, his voice like chips of ice. He made a slight gesture with his hand, and the glacier groaned, moving beneath Johnny's feet.

Johnny had a sudden image of the crevasse closing up and Cheryl being turned into a red smear. "Wait!"

❊ ❊ ❊ ❊

Cheryl tried to climb the lines while waiting for Johnny. She made it up a foot, then slipped and dangled in mid-air for a moment, something that so terrified her she quickly reverted to her sitting on the wall position. "Hurry," she whispered. Her hands were red and stiff. She wasn't sure how much longer she could hold on.

It seemed forever before Johnny's face appeared above her. "Cheryl?"

"Still here," she called up through chattering teeth.

"What command do I give the dogs to make them go forward?" Johnny asked. "We're going to pull you out."

Cheryl gave a sigh of relief. "You disarmed the bomb?"

He didn't answer. "What's the Inuktitut word for 'go'?"

A siren went off in Cheryl's head. "Did you disarm the bomb?"

Johnny looked miserable. "I couldn't. Frost is here. He'll crush you if I don't do what he wants."

"No!"

"I won't let you die."

"I'm dead anyway if the nuke goes off!"

Johnny spoke rapidly. "We won't die, Cheryl. Frost's willing to make a deal. He'll entomb us until the radiation dies out, and we'll wake in a new world. A fresh, clean world with no pollution or crime. We'll be together and that's what matters."

No other people. Just ice and maybe a few one-celled organisms.

"You *can't*," Cheryl said. What could she say to convince him?

"Shadow, go, pull!" Johnny yelled, waving his hands.

Shadow either understood or just did what he wanted to: pull. The gang-line began to move.

Without giving herself a chance to think about it, Cheryl let go of the line and quickly braced herself again. The line disappeared above.

She heard Johnny scream, "No!" and hoped he'd take the bomb apart to spite Frost, but seconds later his head appeared above her again. "Cheryl!"

She said nothing. Her thighs quivered like jello.

"What happened? Did your hands slip? I'm going to lower the line to you again. If it's not long enough, I'll get Frost to—"

"Don't bother," Cheryl told him. "I'm not coming up until you disarm the bomb." The strain in her back, in her thighs and knees was excruciating. She spoke between pants.

Johnny hesitated. "Don't argue, Cheryl. Just grab the line."

"Promise me you'll disarm the bomb."

"Evan's dead," Johnny said at last. There were tears in his eyes. "I can't—I just can't—let you die, too. I can't be alone again. Not even if it means some other people die. I'm sorry."

He didn't know what was going on in the world right now and if she told him it would sound like a lie. She hadn't been paying attention to Kathy and would get something wrong—was it North Korea or South Korea that had attacked the other one? She always mixed up which one was which.

"Grab the line!" Johnny yelled.

"No." *Slipping, slipping.* "Evan's not dead. And even if he was, what about my grandfather and Aunt Wanda? What about Kathy and Minik and Brendan and your aunt and uncle? Are you going to kill them all, just to save me? How could I possibly live with that kind of guilt? I'd rather die now." Maybe she should just let go. Fall. It would be quick, and she couldn't hold on much longer anyway.

Suddenly Frost was there. "If she wishes to die, leave her. The crevasse is closing."

If the crevasse was closing it was because Frost wanted it to.

"No, wait!" Johnny yelled. "Cheryl doesn't want to die. She'll accept your offer. Right, Cheryl?" And then Johnny winked at her.

About to yell that she would rather die than live in Frost's new world, Cheryl paused. He winked again, looking frantic.

He was asking her to trust him. He meant to disarm the bomb after she was safe.

Or was he only pretending to go along with her in order to save her life? Johnny was a trickster. He'd betrayed her trust before, hurt her.

But the terror in his eyes... He loved her. All he'd ever tried to do was keep her safe from Frost.

Suddenly Cheryl was ashamed of how hard the last step was for her to take. To let herself trust him. "I accept!" she screamed. "I want to live!" She grabbed the line.

"Pull!" Johnny yelled at the dogs.

Crack, crack. Ice grinded against ice as the glacier started to push the crevasse back together, and Frost did nothing to stop it.

The tug on the gang-line was immediate and strong. Cheryl gained three feet, but the walls were closing. *So? It makes it easier to climb*, she told herself grimly.

Crackle—grind—scrape.

"Faster!" Johnny yelled at the dogs.

Cheryl lunged, fought, climbed, and gained five more feet. Still eight feet to go. She gasped in another breath and tried again.

CRACK!

The sides pressed in on her, hundreds of tonnes of ice shifting.

Cheryl clawed at the ice walls and fought her way up as if climbing a ladder. Johnny and the dogs pulled hard, popping her up the last five feet like a cork from a bottle, as the crevasse closed with a thunderous clap.

She lay on the ice a moment, breathing hard. Johnny put her cold hands between his.

Frost stood over them. "The bomb will go off soon. I need to entomb you now." He raised his misshapen hands. The nails on them were long and black.

"Wait!" Johnny said. "I need something from my backpack." He skated towards his backpack—and the bomb.

Frost smiled. He didn't realize what Johnny was up to until Johnny grabbed the bomb and ripped out the wires connecting the detonator to the plastique.

Cheryl breathed a sigh of relief. Too soon.

In a flash, Frost was standing in front of Johnny. "Put it back together or I'll kill her."

"Don't listen to him." Cheryl hurried to Johnny's side before Frost could separate them with another crevasse. "If you refuse to be his tool no matter what, he has nothing to gain by killing me."

Except revenge, but Cheryl didn't mention that. She hoped Frost was too cold and emotionless to waste time doing something that didn't serve his ultimate purpose.

Johnny took her hand. "It's okay, Cheryl." He faced Frost fearlessly. "You killed my parents."

Frost didn't deny it. "I've protected you for the last nine years. Sheltered you from pain. Do you really want to give that up? Go back to being naked and vulnerable?"

Johnny turned from him and squeezed Cheryl's hand. "I tried so hard not to let him know I cared about you and Evan. After the polar bear, I broke up with you, and I asked Kathy out even though I knew Evan had a crush on her. I made sure both of you hated me, but it didn't work." He looked at Frost with hatred. "*You made my skate cut Evan's throat.*"

Frost seemed almost puzzled, as if he didn't understand why that would upset Johnny. "You're being foolish. I'll eventually acquire another servant to detonate the nuclear bomb. Humanity is doomed. Why not save yourself?"

"No."

Frost was silent for a moment. Then he looked at their joined hands. "She's the reason you're doing this. You'll change your mind once she's dead."

He vanished.

The wind howled like a beast, and the temperature plunged twenty degrees in the space of a heartbeat.

CHAPTER 19

-40 °C (-40 °F)

FOR KATHY, THE SUDDEN DROP in temperature came without warning. One breath was chill, the next one was cold enough to shock her lungs and freeze the tiny hairs in her nose. She faltered on the trail she'd been jogging along.

It's just a cold front, Kathy told herself, but she didn't really believe it. That sharp a change in temperature felt unnatural.

The wind rose up from nowhere, blowing snow. Not the thick, fuzzy flakes so popular on TV, but tiny wind-driven particles that stung as they hit her face. In moments visibility fell to almost zero. The whole world turned white. Kathy felt like she was walking around inside a cotton ball.

She felt like the only human being in the world. Fear twisted inside her. She could freeze to death out here and no one would find her for days.

Kathy quickly zipped up her gaping jacket, yanked down her balaclava and pulled up her hood. *It doesn't matter if it's minus forty,* she told herself. She wasn't some idiot wearing jeans and sneakers; she was properly dressed for bad weather.

Cheryl would say that Frost had turned the weather. Maybe the plunging temperature meant he was angry. That could be a good sign, meaning that Cheryl had succeeded in reaching Johnny. If the bomb wasn't going to go off, then she didn't need to keep going. She could wait here on the trail for Cheryl and Johnny to pick her up with the dogsled.

The idea was tempting. She was tired. But she didn't know that the storm was caused by Frost, and even if it was his doing she didn't know what was happening with Cheryl and Johnny. Every minute might be bringing the possibility of nuclear war closer.

You can do it. It's just a couple hours of walking to Iqaluit. You'll stay warmer if you're moving anyhow.

Only, in the whiteout she began to have trouble keeping to the sled tracks and had to slow to a walk. Every fifth or sixth step she would accidentally veer off the trampled track and step into unpacked snow. It took precious seconds to find the dogsled track again every time.

It would take her at least half an hour longer to get back to Iqaluit. That meant she'd probably arrive around 2:00 p.m. Anywhere else 2:00 p.m. would have been high afternoon, but Iqaluit was so close to the Arctic Circle that at this time of year sunset was at 1:45 p.m. It wouldn't be completely dark, but the period of twilight would be shortened by the storm.

There's nothing you can do about that. Just keep walking.

Her feet got cold first. She was still wearing last year's boots, and the fake-fur pile had been compacted by sweat. They no longer provided the warmth they once had. She tried to wiggle her toes, but it was awkward while walking and she soon gave up.

Her jacket and ski pants kept most of her warm. Too warm. She began to sweat, and her coat soon crackled with the layer of ice that had formed inside the lining. It was an effort to keep up the pace.

Cold, cold, cold. Kathy knew she should breathe in through her nose to allow the air extra time to warm before reaching the lungs, but time and time again she caught herself breathing through her mouth. Her lungs began to ache.

She was already tired. Although the dogs had pulled her for part of the trip to the glacier, she had run the rest of it and her leg muscles ached.

When her watch said noon, Kathy allowed herself to stop and rest. She knelt in the snow and almost cried in relief. She was so cold and tired, she wanted to sit down for a week.

Instead she rested for five minutes then walked back into the storm. She gave herself a pep talk. *You can do this. The fate of the world may be depending on you. You have to do it.* She pictured her father's face, encouraging her, cheering her on as he had at every school track meet. He believed in her. When she told him, at age nine, that she wanted to be a fighter jet pilot he had sat her down and explained carefully what exactly that would mean, the physical training, the competition, the high marks needed. Then, when she hadn't changed her mind, he had hugged her and told her she could do it.

Kathy took a step forward into knee-deep snow. Damn it, she was off the track again. She stepped back—and still couldn't find it.

Where was it? Kathy began to panic, her heart sounding unnaturally loud in her ears, but she made herself stand still in the whirling blizzard and feel for the path with an outstretched foot.

She couldn't find it. Her heart did jumping jacks until she realized what had happened. The dogsled track was still there, dead ahead of her, but the wind had had enough time to start to blow it in. Drifts were forming. She had walked into one, that was all.

The drifts started small, but soon began to get bigger.

Kathy could remember trudging through drifts as a child, breaking a trail, and having fun, playing explorer in an uncharted world, but that had been for half an hour. She had now been walking for close to an hour, in intense cold, straight into the wind. It wasn't fun; it was grim work.

Doubts crept in. What if she couldn't make it back to Iqaluit? Better outdoorsmen than she had gotten lost in blizzards and wandered helplessly until succumbing to hypothermia.

Would it be better to stay here on the trail, conserve energy, and not risk wandering in circles? If she mistakenly wandered onto the sea ice they'd never find her. She was afraid of dying.

You have a duty to keep going.

Half an hour later Kathy finally admitted that she'd lost the path entirely. She'd had her eyes closed against the sting of snow and had been walking in a kind of numb trance. She had no idea where she'd left the trail, if it had been five minutes ago or half an hour.

Should she go back, retrace her steps and find the trail again?

It was the logical thing to do, but Kathy didn't trust herself to be able to find the track again. It would be almost totally drifted over by now. Kathy could no longer fool herself that this was just a storm. It felt too personal. Frost was her opponent; he'd pitted his storm against her, pushing her—

Pushing. If she kept the wind directly in her face, she would know she was going in the direction Frost didn't want her to go.

While she turned the logic over in her mind, Kathy sat down for a break. Her stomach growled, but had to be satisfied with several handfuls of snow. The survival books all said to melt the snow before drinking it, so you don't lose body heat melting it in your mouth, but Kathy had no wood here above the treeline, no matches, no container and no choice. She swallowed the last mouthful of snow, got up and trudged on.

She slitted her eyes and peered through the white veil of snow, but could still see no smoke or any sign of human habitation.

The tops of her cheeks, even under the protection of the balaclava, were beginning to feel numb with cold. Kathy tugged off her snowmobile mitts and pressed her gloved hands over the cold spots as she walked until she could feel them again.

The breaks she took started to get more and more frequent. 1:10. 1:35. 1:45. Each time it was harder to get started again.

You have a duty to your country.

Daylight was fading fast. Frost was winning.

Kathy shivered. A bad sign. It meant her muscles were spasming in a desperate attempt to produce more heat. But the more she shivered the less energy she would have to maintain her body temperature. So she would shiver more. Shivering was the beginning of the end.

Kathy stifled her shivers and clamped her jaw tight shut to prevent her teeth from chattering. She felt lightheaded, drowsy. It was difficult to walk in a straight line. The wind pushed her, and she swayed on her feet, leaning into it.

When the wind suddenly stopped, she almost fell. The snow stopped blowing. She could see. Kathy raised her head and saw The Stranger. She was standing with him in a small circle of calm.

"Hello, Stranger. Oops, I mean, Frost." Kathy put her hands over her mouth, stifling a giggle. She must be more light-headed than she'd realized.

Frost stood on top of the snow, his feet not sinking in even a little. He gave the impression of wearing clothes, but whenever she tried to look at them straight on, they blurred. She couldn't tell if he wore blue jeans or fur. His ivory skin looked tougher than leather. He looked old. So old. She was an ant to him, a bug, Kathy realized. His black eyes seemed to swallow her up.

"You won't make it," he said. Outside of their little circle the wind was howling, but he didn't even have to raise his voice. "You're lost, wandering in circles. You will freeze to death within fifteen minutes."

Kathy almost told him she wasn't going in circles; she was walking into the wind to keep straight. She kept the words back only by strong effort.

Her legs trembled, but she made herself walk forward.

"Today is the winter solstice, the shortest day of the year," Frost said in a cold clear voice. "The sun set ten minutes ago. Soon it will be completely dark." He waved a four-fingered hand at the graying horizon.

Kathy walked right past him.

"You're cold and in pain," he said from behind her. "I can save you—if you do a small task for me in turn."

Kathy wanted to say something—*fate of the world—her duty— couldn't let her dad down*—but her mind was so cold and leaden she couldn't form a complete sentence.

She kept walking. When she reached the border between calm and blizzard, she hesitated. Every fiber of her being protested reentering the maelstrom. She wanted to stay here and sleep.

Fate of the world.

Duty.

It took all her courage to step through. The circle of quiet was broken and the wind descended on her like a demon. Cold scythed through her. She wanted, desperately, to turn around and go back to Frost's oasis.

She walked.

The last bit of twilight had bled from the world when she bumped into stone.

At first Kathy thought it was a wall, a building, but further, clumsy exploration with her hands showed that it wasn't. It was stone piled tall in the shape of a man. A monument. A landmark. Name of her school. What was the word? It was an Inuit word. Monument. Landmark. Place of power.

Inuksuk. That was it. It was an inuksuk. The identification of the stone landmark pleased Kathy immensely, though she could not, at the moment, think why.

Cheryl would know why it was important. Too bad Cheryl wasn't here. Too bad. Too bad.

Thinking about Cheryl made Kathy remember the muktuk Cheryl had given her. Cheryl had said it would make her warm. It took Kathy several minutes of fumbling to retrieve the package she'd put in her pocket and stuff the whale blubber through the frosty slit in her balaclava into her mouth. She chewed, swallowed. It wasn't so bad. She took another bite.

Warmth. Incredible warmth radiating from her skin. Kathy ate all the muktuk. Her mind cleared, and she thought she knew where she might be. There was an inuksuk not far from the airbase.

She turned in a slow circle, looking for the airbase. In the sea of darkness a flicker of light caught her eye. "Ol' Jackie didn't want me to see. He knew I was getting close," she mumbled to herself.

The light didn't look very far away, maybe only a mile, but lights could be deceptive in the dark.

Slap. As soon as Kathy stepped out from behind the tall inuksuk, the full force of the wind hit her.

Kathy began to walk. She tired swiftly, the energy from the muktuk draining away. Her feet moved listlessly. She was so tired....

She kept tripping, exhaustion dulling her normal reflexes. She sank to her knees in the snow. Cold, so cold... She would just lie down for a minute and rest.

The wind blew with awesome force, howling around her. It shrieked and bellowed and in its roar she heard Frost's laugh.

Panic kicked in her chest, dislodging the gray stone of weariness. If she didn't get up now, she'd never get up again.

She got up.

Fate of... fate of something. Somebody depending on her. Duty.

Kathy walked towards the light, until it winked out.

She stopped, but only for a moment. She had no choice, but to keep plodding in the same direction, so she did, limbs numb.

At one point she found herself sitting in a snow bank and wondering how she got there. *Better get up*, she said to *herself*. Her legs didn't move. *Come on legs, get up.* They didn't move. *Darn. Guess*

I'll just have to stay here. Kathy lay back in the snow looking up at the black sky.

She remembered making snow angels as a kid and flopped her arms and legs, making wings. Pretty angel. Too bad she couldn't get up and see it. Her legs wouldn't move. *But they just had, making the snow angel.* Somehow that thought didn't make her happy. It meant she had to get up again.

Kathy rolled onto her knees, wrecking the angel, and staggered up. She began to plod forward again. One foot in front of the other. For awhile she tried counting her steps, but she kept getting confused. *One, two, three, four, five, seven, eleven. No, that wasn't right. She tried again. One, two, four, six, eight, who do we appreciate?*

Kathy opened her eyes and saw the light. She stopped, stupefied. She had just enough sense left to reason that it had been hidden behind the hill she'd just climbed.

There were many lights now, forming two rows. Kathy started to walk between them, and a light appeared directly in front of her. Was the light heaven? It would be warm in heaven. She tried to smile, and her lips cracked. She tasted blood, but didn't care.

The light got bigger, and Kathy heard a throaty, growling noise, a noise she should know. Kathy squinted, standing still as the light rushed towards her, engines labouring.

It was a plane—and she was standing in the middle of the runway.

Kathy threw herself flat just as the CF-18's wing passed over her. The backwash of air from its passage tumbled her over like a feather.

She was still lying there when the ground crew found her.

❄ ❄ ❄ ❄

On her way to the hospital Kathy roused enough to ask for her father. *Fate of the world...*

"He'll see you at the hospital later," the army med tech told her, busily strapping her down to a gurney. "We're a little busy right now."

"No." Kathy grasped the med tech's wrist before she could strap Kathy's hand down, too. "It's important. I have military information." She fell back, exhausted.

The med tech looked doubtful, but got her father.

Her dad's tired face seem to age another five years when he saw her. "Oh, Kathy." He sat beside her and held her cold hands. "They told me you had hypothermia. What happened? Why aren't you at home? What were you doing out in this weather?"

Kathy's head was swimming. She tried to come up with a story that didn't implicate Johnny. "Johnny saw something suspicious... last night. Cheryl and I followed him out onto the tundra. We found the wreckage from the lost plane..."

She could see that her dad wasn't following. She had to make him understand. She squeezed his hand as hard as she could. "An old plane wreck, a Russian stealth plane. It had a nuke... a missile. There was a bomb." Who was supposed to have brought the bomb? She couldn't come up with a good lie, pressed on. "You have to tell NORAD. If there's an explosion, it's not North Korea." Her dad sat straight up, galvanized. "I walked for hours. Johnny and Cheryl are still out there. Please find them."

"I will."

Her dad left, and Kathy lay back on the bed. In spite of her exhaustion, she smiled. She felt like Laura Secord or the man who'd first run the Iditarod to bring needed medicines to a town. She'd accomplished her mission even though she'd had to risk her life to do it. When the time came to join the Armed Forces, she could do it with a glad heart, without doubt. She'd proved something to herself today. She had what it took.

Kathy closed her eyes and slid into sleep.

❄ ❄ ❄ ❄

The next face Kathy saw was her mother's. Kathy tried to speak, but only a croak came out.

Her mother understood and answered anyway. "The Americans have destroyed North Korea's nuclear capabilities. The alert is over."

Kathy kept looking at her, silently asking for more news.

"Pat Vander Zee phoned. She says Evan is recovering from surgery and the doctors think he's out of danger."

"Johnny?" Kathy croaked when her mom didn't go on.

Her mother looked away, and fear gonged in Kathy's heart. "The Emergency Measures Office in Iqaluit and your dad are coordinating a search and rescue, but with the storm and the temperature below -40 °C... Once it's dawn, they'll have a better chance of finding them."

Or their bodies, Kathy thought. She lay back on the bed and stared up at the ceiling, trying not to cry.

CHAPTER 20

-43 °C (-45 °F)

COLD. CHERYL THOUGHT she'd been cold before, but now she felt as if she'd been dipped in ice. This cold meant Death.

Cheryl quickly stuffed her hands into the waistband of her ski-pants before the wind could freeze sections of her skin. Quickly, she and Johnny backtracked her trail and Cheryl put back on the clothing she had discarded: coat, scarf, balaclava.

All except her sealskin mitts. All they found was one pathetic wool glove with a hole in one finger.

"Where are your mitts?" Johnny asked, raising his voice to be heard over the howl of the wind.

Cheryl remembered tossing them onto the dogsled. They must have fallen over the edge with everything else. "Down in the crevasse."

"Here, wrap your hand in my scarf. We've got to get off this glacier." Ominous cracking sounds confirmed Johnny's words.

They were in deep trouble. The loss of Cheryl's mitts was bad enough, but, as always, Johnny was not dressed warmly enough for the cold. Only this time Frost might not protect him. His head was bare, his jacket had no hood and his ears were rapidly turning red. Cheryl forced him to put on her balaclava; the fur ruff on her hood and her scarf would protect most of her face.

Cheryl bound her bare hand carefully in Johnny's scarf and made a fist of her other hand so the hole in the glove wasn't exposed. She was still shivering. "What about the bomb?"

Johnny skated over to it and hurled the alarm clock away, but seemed less certain what to do with the plastique. "I don't want to leave it here, so close to the nuke. Frost can't light the fuse himself, he's not solid enough, but he might get another minion."

"Take it with us," Cheryl hollered, jiggling in place to get warm.

Johnny put the plastique back in his backpack and began to skate back towards Cheryl.

The smooth-as-glass surface of the glacier heaved under them, sending them both to their knees, and became a frozen sea with three-foot waves.

"He's going to make things difficult," Johnny said grimly as he unlaced his skates with clumsy mittened fingers. He removed his boots from his backpack and quickly put them on.

You mean he's going to try to kill me, Cheryl thought.

The wind shrieked angrily, its touch like whips flaying skin.

"Come on!" Johnny yelled, getting to his feet.

While the glacier continued to shift and crack and moan beneath them, the giant waking, Cheryl got the dogs and sled turned around. The dogs were eager to go, and she ran behind them. Johnny stayed within touching distance of Cheryl. If another crevasse opened, it would take both of them.

The wind blew loose snow directly in her face, making her eyes tear. The tears, in turn, froze to her eyelashes. She ran blindly, trusting the dogs.

They reached the edge of the glacier and stood for a moment looking down. As she watched, the glacier reformed itself moment by moment, retreating. "How do we get down?" Cheryl yelled into the wind.

Johnny didn't hesitate. "Sit on your bum and slide."

Before Cheryl could protest that the foot of the glacier was way too steep and bumpy for that, Johnny pulled her down. He sat in front of her, her legs on either side of his. "We go down together!" he yelled and pushed off. Down the steep slope.

Cheryl clenched her teeth on a scream and held on tight, sick to her stomach, certain they were going to die, but Johnny knew Frost better than her. "He needs me alive," Johnny shouted as they slid faster and faster.

Cheryl peeked out through slitted eyelids, saw an upcoming bump just before they went airborne for two feet, and slammed her eyes shut again. Better not to see.

Then her feet plowed through snow. They were down. Safe. Cheryl went limp with relief.

Then she heard howling. "The dogs!" She turned and saw that the dogs were already halfway down, running sure-footedly. The dogsled took a terrible beating, but made it to the bottom, too.

Cheryl hauled herself shakily to her feet and took stock. The dogs were fine, but the sled was broken. They were miles out of town, the temperature was at least –40 °C plus wind-chill and the blizzard was too thick to see in. Johnny was shivering in his jeans and short coat. Cheryl would have bet money the idiot wasn't even wearing long underwear.

She regretted once more the blankets that had fallen into the crevasse.

"We have to find shelter," Cheryl yelled over the wind.

"Where?" Johnny yelled back. Despair grooved his face, but he didn't mention Frost's offer to preserve them.

Normally the immense bulk of the glacier would have provided some, but Cheryl didn't want to risk camping in its shadow and having a wall of ice shear off and fall on them. She walked over to the dogsled.

For as long as she could remember her grandfather had carried a snow knife strapped to the dogsled's frame. She just prayed it hadn't fallen into the crevasse along with everything else.

Without a snow knife she and Johnny would die.

It was there. Cheryl let out the breath she had been holding, as she pulled out the long, flat piece of bone. She spoke with confidence. "We have to build a snow house."

"You mean an igloo?" Johnny asked.

In Inuktitut all houses were called igloos and a snow house was called an igluvigak, but Cheryl did not bother to correct him. She nodded. Two people could build a snow house in an hour.

"How?"

"First we have to find the right kind of snow. Tundra snow." Cheryl had never actually built a snow house on her own —her grandfather had always helped—and she found herself unconsciously instructing Johnny as her grandfather had always instructed her. The slow steps calmed her.

"What's tundra snow?"

Cheryl began to walk, casting about for a good spot. Tundra snow was harder than regular snow, wind-packed, and the snow had to come from a single snowfall so that the blocks she cut from it had no cracks. "Here," she said, squatting. "This is tundra snow."

Johnny crouched beside her to look. Ice cracked and fell from his jeans.

"First we make a circle." Cheryl marked a small six-foot one in the snow, packing it down with her boots. "Then I cut blocks from the center."

The first blocks were the largest and most important. Grandfather had always cut them, and Johnny's gaze made Cheryl nervous. "You unharness the dogs while I cut the blocks."

As soon as Johnny unharnessed Shadow she dug a hole in the snow and curled up for the night. Her fur would keep her warm, and she placed her curly tail over her nose to shield her lungs from the cold air. The other dogs copied her.

The dogs would be fine. It was the humans who were in trouble. Cheryl took a deep breath and made the first cut. She cut two blocks close to three feet in length, two feet wide and half a foot thick, then called Johnny over to help her.

They lifted the 40-pound block of snow out of its hole and laid it on its side along the perimeter she had marked out. The second block joined it.

Johnny finished unharnessing the dogs while she cut more blocks. Cheryl was alarmed to note that her hands, in their inadequate wrappings, were already freezing. She put them in her pockets for a few minutes, flexing and unflexing them to keep the blood moving, but they were slow to uncurl.

Once they had a circle of blocks laid on their sides, it was time to use the snow knife again. Cheryl started at the bottom left corner of one block and cut upwards at a slight angle while moving along the circle and finally ending at the top right-hand corner of the snow block to the left of the one where she'd started. She went round one more time, carefully shaving the new diagonal line so that it slanted inward.

After that, the pattern would just continue. More snow blocks laid on top of the first row, spiraling upwards and slanting inwards, forming a dome.

It was cold, cold work done in the teeth of the storm. Pins and needles pricked her hands, both glove and the scarf soon wet and useless. Cheryl kept having to stop and warm her hands in her pockets—once she went and warmed them in Shadow's fur. The growing walls protected her a little, but no matter which way she turned Frost kept the wind in her face.

Johnny started to stumble on his frozen legs, but Frost must still have been partially protecting him or he would have been in much worse shape.

Dead.

Just over an hour had passed when it was finally time to lay the keystone. Since Johnny was taller, he stayed outside to hand her the snow block, while Cheryl tunneled an entrance into the snow house below the first row of blocks.

The cessation of wind inside the dome felt like a benediction from heaven. Cheryl wanted nothing more than to lie there and bask in it, but Johnny was still out in the cold wind, so she forced herself to stand in the pit and wave her scarf-clad hand through the hole at the top of the dome. "I'm ready."

The keystone didn't come.

"Johnny!" Cheryl shouted.

The wind brought her snatches of a voice that wasn't Johnny's.

The thought of rescue flickered through her mind, then winked out as she recognized Frost's voice.

❄ ❄ ❄ ❄

"Johnny, Johnny." Frost's voice was full of mocking sadness. "Do you really think this puny structure will protect you from me? A house made of snow, my element? I've been lenient so far—"

Lenient? Johnny could barely feel his legs, he felt like some kind of lurching Frankenstein whenever he tried to walk and he was worried about Cheryl's hands. But the igloo was almost finished. "Give up," he told Frost. "You lost."

"If you go inside there, I promise you it will be your tomb." Black certainty weighted Frost's words like cold iron.

Ice, creeping everywhere. Johnny tried to shake it off, but the fatigue pulling at his muscles made it harder. "I won't do it," Johnny said, but his voice came out leaden, without conviction. "I won't set off your bomb."

"Ice is your element, too. Think of how much you love hockey," Frost argued.

"Johnny, the keystone." The words were faint, whipped away by the wind.

Frost's wind.

Johnny blinked. There was something wrong... "Just because I love skating doesn't mean I'm like you," he told Frost. He had a sudden realization. "You want me to be like you: alone. But I'm not. There are people that I love and people that love me." Even when he didn't deserve it. Johnny figured he owed most of them an apology.

"You've been my creature for eight years. You're more like me than you think," Frost said. His black eyes glittered with... triumph?

But Frost was losing. The igloo was almost done. It would shelter Cheryl and keep her alive. Johnny only had to place the keystone, and it would be over. Johnny's heart began to beat faster.

"Johnny..." The wind rose again, swallowing Cheryl's words. Her warning.

"You're trying to keep me talking until she freezes to death," Johnny said, horrified.

Frost said something more, but Johnny ignored him, lifting the keystone. Cheryl's hands poked out of the hole in the igloo, and he lowered the keystone carefully in place, into her hands.

But Frost had one more thing to say before Johnny crawled inside the igloo to safety, words that made Johnny's victory seem hollow: "Rescue isn't coming. Your friend froze to death and in a few days so will this one."

Johnny tried to tell himself Frost was lying, but it would be very easy for Kathy to get lost in the blizzard and freeze in a snowbank somewhere. Her chances of making it were low, probably only one in five.

"He might be lying," Cheryl said. She'd heard, too.

"He might." Johnny hugged her for comfort and warmth.

He'd thought they were done, but a few moments later Cheryl wriggled free. "There are still a few more things to do. Most igluvigaks have small tunnels shielding the entrance, but we don't have time for that. Bring in Samwise and we'll plug the whole entrance off with a snow block."

Johnny looked around the small interior of the igloo and had a sinking realization. "The rest of the dogs—there isn't room for them. What about Shadow? We might be able to fit two dogs," he said desperately. Cheryl's grandfather had invested years training Shadow; he was more important than Samwise.

But Cheryl was shaking her head. "The dogs will be fine. They're born for this kind of weather. We need Samwise's body heat, not the other way around. I know it sounds cruel, but it really isn't. In the old times dogs were only allowed inside to have puppies, and they survived quite well in all weather."

Johnny still felt doubtful, but supposed the other arctic animals like polar bears didn't get to crawl inside an igloo.

"You get Samwise, I'll cut the snow plug," Cheryl said. She tried to pick up the snow knife, but dropped it. Part of the scarf had come unwrapped and bare skin showed.

"Cheryl!" Johnny was horrified at the sight of her fingers, which were no longer white and cold, but red and swollen.

Cheryl looked down at her hands and said calmly, "I guess you'll have to do it then."

"Here, take my mittens." Johnny pulled them off.

She refused. "Not until you put the snowblock in place. I've already got frostbite. If you take off your mitts, we'll both have frostbite."

He swore, but could see from her face that arguing with her would just waste time. "Okay, but stay inside." He crawled back out, found Samwise's white shape in the snow and forced the at-first-whiny-then-happy dog inside. Samwise made straight for Cheryl, licking her face.

Johnny backed out again and made quick work of cutting a block and dragging it back in behind him.

"Anything else we can do?" he asked, throwing the mitts at her.

Cheryl lacked the coordination to pull the mitts on, and Johnny had to help her while she pondered his question. "Heat rises. We should sit on the higher part of the floor, not in the trough where I cut the first blocks from."

They heaved themselves up onto the ground level, but the dome was so small they had to hold each other lying down. Samwise settled in at their backs. "A true igluvigak would have a snow platform on one side to sleep on," Cheryl told him, "preferably on top of skins, but this will have to do."

Outside the wind howled. Johnny listened nervously. "Frost said an igloo couldn't protect us."

In the scattered light filtering through the snow walls, Cheryl smiled faintly. "He can huff and puff all he likes, but he won't blow our snow house down. He'll just make it stronger."

"How?" Johnny asked, puzzled.

"It's the dome shape. When the wind sweeps over and around the snow house, it presses down. The snow compresses and gets stronger. He's actually doing us a favour."

Her words surprised Johnny into a true laugh. "I won't tell him, if you won't."

"Now be silent," Cheryl told him tenderly. "In a snow house you must think small. Grandfather always says to move as little as possible and expend no energy. Pretend you're a bear hibernating for the winter."

Johnny smiled and they lay together, resting and gradually warming as the last light faded and the long, long winter night began.

❄ ❄ ❄ ❄

The sound of snowmobile engines woke them. Johnny quickly unblocked the plugged doorway and crawled out, frantically waving his hands.

The storm was over, the day clear, and the leader of the snowmobiles saw him and immediately started driving toward him. Rescue was here.

Johnny was so relieved it took him until Cheryl gasped and pointed to realize that the glacier had retreated back out of sight. Johnny did not doubt that Frost had pulled it all the way back to the ice field where it belonged—and taken the lost plane and its nuclear missile with it. Biding his time.

CHAPTER 21

-17 °C (+2 °F)

THE NEXT TWO DAYS passed in a blur of doctors. They treated Cheryl for hypothermia and frostbite. She wasn't alone: Kathy and Johnny also put in hospital time. Kathy had gotten off the lightest, with only a small patch of frostbite below her left eye. Johnny had large patches on his legs. Frost had marked all of them, but Cheryl the worst. The skin on her left hand blackened in spots, a sign of gangrene, and two of the fingers had to be amputated.

The loss made simple things like eating and holding a pen awkward, but Cheryl held hard to her gratitude at being alive. "The marks are a badge," she told Kathy one day when Kathy and Johnny were visiting her and Kathy expressed concern. "They are a sign that we fought Frost and won. It could so easily have gone the other way."

"I know what you mean," Kathy said fervently. "The crisis is over, but I'm still scared. We stopped Frost this time, but what about next time?"

"He will try again," Cheryl agreed. She turned to Johnny. "Won't he?"

"We've bought some time," Johnny said. "It took Frost ten years to cultivate me into his pawn. He put his mark on me when I was a child and still able to believe. Most kids these days have barely heard of Jack Frost."

"Will he really start over from scratch? What if Frost tries something desperate?" Kathy asked.

Johnny shrugged. "I don't know, but I doubt it. You have to understand: Frost thinks in terms of millennia. All he has to do is bide his time and wait, and eventually the ice will come again."

Cheryl decided she could live with that.

On Christmas Eve, the day before she was released, Cheryl had a special visitor. Evan. His throat was still bandaged, but he could talk clearly and was on his feet, back from Ottawa.

"You know, sympathy is all well and good," Evan said, sitting down, "but all three of you didn't have to put yourself in the hospital just because I did."

Cheryl smiled. "What did Johnny say when he saw you? He was convinced that he'd killed you."

Evan swallowed and had to look away. "He cried. He hugged me and told me he loved me and that he was sorry about his skate."

"What did you say?"

"I told him it was okay; it was just an accident."

"Good." Cheryl couldn't say any more. Her throat closed with emotion. She wished she had been there to see their reunion.

"Actually," Evan said after a long pause. "Johnny was why I came down here to talk to you."

"Oh?" A cold finger touched Cheryl's heart. Johnny had all but lived in her room when he was hospitalized and even since he had been well enough to go home, he had visited twice a day, bearing different gifts each time: chocolates, puzzle books, a journal to write her poetry in and a rainbow of pens, one colour for every mood. Johnny had seemed his usual self to Cheryl: outrageous and fun.

"Uncle Dan arranged for him to play junior hockey in Ontario," Evan said. "But Johnny's refusing to go. Aunt Pat says he hasn't practiced hockey once since getting out of the hospital. I would have thought the arena was the first place he'd go."

"And you want to know if it's because of me, if he doesn't want to leave his girlfriend behind," Cheryl finished for him. Evan blushed, but didn't deny it. "I don't know," she told Evan. "I'll talk to him."

"Thanks." Evan left shortly afterward.

Cheryl was selfish enough that the thought of Johnny going away to play hockey in Ontario depressed her, but she knew she would feel much worse if he gave up his dream to stay with her. Especially if he was motivated, even a little bit, out of guilt for her two lost fingers. She decided to have it out with him the instant he came to visit her.

Her resolve melted away when Johnny came into her room that evening carrying a huge black and white teddy bear with a red bow around his neck.

"Merry Christmas. It's a panda, not a polar bear," he said. "They're vegetarians."

"Thank you," Cheryl said. She had never had a stuffed animal before and this one was nearly as big as she was. It was also cute. "Does he have a name?" She rubbed her face in the bear's plush fur and kissed its nose.

She expected Johnny to tease her about being jealous of his own bear, but instead he said quite abruptly, "You asked me once if I would run away if we saw the polar bear again. I won't. I love you."

A great knot eased around Cheryl's heart. "I love you, too." She abandoned the panda bear and wordlessly pulled Johnny's head down to meet her lips. The angle must have been uncomfortable for him, but he kissed her back eagerly. The kiss was sweeter somehow, more honest, than any of their previous kisses. A new beginning.

They sat with their hands linked for several minutes before Cheryl decided to tackle the next problem. "Evan says you haven't been skating. Is it because of his accident?" Cheryl didn't wait for Johnny's reply. "For the last time, Frost caused it, not you. You have to stop wallowing in guilt."

"I'm not wallowing in guilt." Johnny looked up, and Cheryl saw fear in his eyes. The fear he was now willing to let her see.

"Then why aren't you going to play on the junior team in Ontario?"

"Evan told you that, too, huh? What a tattletale," Johnny said without heat.

"Is it because of me? We can still e-mail each other and talk on the phone even if you move to Ontario." Cheryl would miss him, but she knew that they wouldn't be separated forever.

She knew Johnny loved her and would never hurt her.

"It's not because of you."

Cheryl began to get impatient. "Then what is it? *Tell me.* Don't shut me out again."

"All right." Johnny shuddered. "It's not what Frost tried to do to Evan; it's what he did to me."

Cheryl thought about that for a moment, but didn't get it. "Freezing your heart? I unthawed that, remember?"

Johnny wasn't in a joking mood. "He turned me into a hockey player. Before my parents drowned, I was just an average player. I didn't start scoring goals until Frost marked me as his own."

Johnny paused. Then he confessed his most secret fear, "Cheryl, what if I can't? Can't skate, can't score, can't play hockey? What will I do?"

"The same thing you'd do if you got injured," Cheryl smiled. "You'd find something else to do. But you won't have to, because you can skate, and you can score. Listen to me, Johnny." Cheryl put all the confidence she could muster into her voice. "Evan told Kathy and me that after your parents died you stayed outside for hours, skating. Maybe Frost helped you endure the cold, but it was those hours and hours of practice that made you a good hockey player. You haven't lost those hours, Johnny. Your muscles know what to do even if your mind is a little scared. Now go tell your uncle you're going to play hockey!"

Johnny stood, then hesitated for a moment in the doorway. "All those years, Frost pushed me to play hockey, because he thought it would make me more like him, cold and alone. But there's something he never understood."

"What?" Cheryl asked.

Johnny grinned a Johnny-grin. "Hockey is a team sport."